NAKED TARGET

Skye Fargo wasn't a fool. He knew Buddy might be leading him into a trap. When they arrived at their destination, he stuck a gun into Buddy's back and told him not to move.

Fargo saw a man step from the trees, a gun in his hand. "Let Buddy go, and we'll talk," the man shouted.

"I don't think so," Fargo answered. "Buddy makes a good shield."

"Not anymore," the man said.

"No, Jesus . . ." Buddy screamed, but his words were cut short as five shots exploded from the trees. Fargo shuddered as Buddy seemed to gyrate in place before he crumpled to the ground. Fargo cursed silently as he stood completely exposed, a helpless target, and watched three other gunmen emerge.

"Christ, he was your own man," Fargo shouted.

He didn't have to ask who was going down next. . . .

**BE SURE TO READ THE OTHER BOOKS
IN THE EXCITING TRAILSMAN SERIES!**

Ø **SIGNET**

TRAILSMAN SERIES BY JON SHARPE

- ☐ THE TRAILSMAN #161: ROGUE RIVER FEUD (182189—$3.99)
- ☐ THE TRAILSMAN #162: REVENGE AT LOST CREEK (182197—$3.99)
- ☐ THE TRAILSMAN #163: YUKON MASSACRE (182200—$3.99)
- ☐ THE TRAILSMAN #164: NEZ PERCE NIGHTMARE (182219—$3.99)
- ☐ THE TRAILSMAN #165: DAKOTA DEATH HOUSE (182227—$4.50)
- ☐ THE TRAILSMAN #166: COLORADO CARNAGE (182235—$4.50)
- ☐ THE TRAILSMAN #167: BLACK MESA TREACHERY (182243—$4.50)
- ☐ THE TRAILSMAN #168: KIOWA COMMAND (185153—$4.50)
- ☐ THE TRAILSMAN #169: SOCORRO SLAUGHTER (185234—$4.99)
- ☐ THE TRAILSMAN #170: UTAH TRACKDOWN (185382—$4.99)
- ☐ THE TRAILSMAN #171: DEAD MAN'S RIVER (185390—$4.99)
- ☐ THE TRAILSMAN #172: SUTTER'S SECRET (185404—$4.99)
- ☐ THE TRAILSMAN #173: WASHINGTON WARPATH (185412—$4.99)
- ☐ THE TRAILSMAN #174: DEATH VALLEY BLOODBATH (185420—$4.99)
- ☐ THE TRAILSMAN #175: BETRAYAL AT EL DIABLO (186672—$4.99)
- ☐ THE TRAILSMAN #176: CURSE OF THE GRIZZLY (186893—$4.99)
- ☐ THE TRAILSMAN #177: COLORADO WOLFPACK (187598—$4.99)
- ☐ THE TRAILSMAN #178: APACHE ARROWS (186680—$4.99)

Prices slightly higher in Canada.

THE TRAILSMAN

179

SAGEBRUSH SKELETONS

by

Jon Sharpe

A SIGNET BOOK

SIGNET
Published by the Penguin Group
Penguin Books USA Inc., 375 Hudson Street,
New York, New York 10014, U.S.A.
Penguin Books Ltd, 27 Wrights Lane,
London W8 5TZ, England
Penguin Books Australia Ltd, Ringwood,
Victoria, Australia
Penguin Books Canada Ltd, 10 Alcorn Avenue,
Toronto, Ontario, Canada M4V 3B2
Penguin Books (N.Z.) Ltd, 182–190 Wairau Road,
Auckland 10, New Zealand

Penguin Books Ltd, Registered Offices:
Harmondsworth, Middlesex, England

First published by Signet, an imprint of Dutton Signet,
a division of Penguin Books USA Inc.

First Printing, November, 1996
10 9 8 7 6 5 4 3 2 1

The first chapter of this book originally appeared in *Apache Arrows,*
the one hundred seventy-eighth volume in this series.

 REGISTERED TRADEMARK—MARCA REGISTRADA

Printed in the United States of America

The Trailsman

Beginnings . . . they bend the tree and they mark the man. Skye Fargo was born when he was eighteen. Terror was his midwife, vengeance his first cry. Killing spawned Skye Fargo, ruthless, cold-blooded murder. Out of the acrid smoke of gunpowder still hanging in the air, he rose, cried out a promise never forgotten.

The Trailsman they began to call him all across the West: searcher, scout, hunter, the man who could see where others only looked, his skills for hire but not his soul, the man who lived each day to the fullest, yet trailed each tomorrow. Skye Fargo, the Trailsman, and the seeker who could take the wildness of a land and the wanting of a woman and make them his own.

1860, South Dakota,
where out of the shadow of
the Black Hills, old skeletons
rise up to bring new deaths . . .

1

The brilliant red of blood suddenly spattered the yellow-gold field of dandelions and streaked the dark green of downy bromegrass. Screams punctuated the warm stillness of the soft, lush valley and the wagons, two Conestogas and one high-sided, converted hay wagon, rolled to an abrupt halt. The first one to see the attackers was Mabel Kotchins. She was in the last wagon, sitting next to her husband, who half dozed as he held the reins, letting the horses follow the wagon ahead of him. Mabel, a big woman wearing a long black dress, screamed as she half rose from the wagon seat. An arrow ended her scream, going all the way through her neck to come out the other side, and Mabel Kotchins toppled headfirst from the wagon.

It was an automatic response that made her husband pull the wagons to a halt as he sat, transfixed for a moment, staring at his wife as she fell to the ground. He was still holding the reins, still staring down at Mabel, when three arrows slammed into him from two directions. With his last moment of life, he saw the attackers racing around to the other side of the three wagons. They had burst from the stand of box elder that rose, tall and dense, alongside where the wagons slowly rolled across the fertile landscape of the eastern Colorado territory. The near-naked riders raced from the trees with blinding speed, hurling clusters of arrows as they did, racing up and down the line of wagons. They indulged in a frenzy of killing that ended only when the last victim, a woman carrying a young towheaded child in her arms, lay crumpled and riddled with arrows alongside the rear wheel of one of the Conestogas. The child also carried two arrows in its small body.

Only then did the attackers halt and dismount. They instantly began to go through the three wagons, tossing the contents out of each, then tearing open each sack, box, and crate. Wooden bureaus were thrown to the ground, each drawer pulled out and every item inside carefully examined. Finally, when the entire contents of the three wagons lay scattered all around the grisly scene, they returned to their horses and raced away, riding a few hundred yards across the open ground before disappearing back into the forest of box elder.

Only a terrible silence remained, and it seemed that even the birds refused to sing and the wind declined to blow. The ferocious attack hadn't taken very long, and now it was over. But it was an end that was also a beginning, more than anybody knew.

Skye Fargo let his smoothly muscled torso turn in Cindy Smith's arms as she half giggled with pleasure. Cindy always giggled when she was enjoying herself. She also reveled in physical touch, skin against skin, the tender stimuli of hair, eyelashes, lips. That had stayed the same, an echo of those days when he knew her back in that little town down Kansas way. Cindy half giggled again as she rubbed shallow yet so very soft breasts over his face, then paused to let his lips gently pull on each. "It took you long enough to come visit," she said, reproach in her tone.

"It wasn't for not thinking about you. I just haven't come out to this part of Colorado territory," Fargo said, the answer completely true. He'd had good times with Cindy back in Kansas, and he'd been sorry when she picked up stakes and followed her folks out to this new frontier. Her pa had opened a business, a general store, in Dennison near the army post, and Cindy had begun her own enterprise as a seamstress. The little cabin where they lay naked on a bedstead covered with a thick blanket had been purchased from an old miner and she used it as a hideaway of her own. "No trouble from the tribes out this far from town?" Fargo had asked.

"No. The Ponca, Oto, and Kansa are the tribes around here, and they're pretty peaceful. The bad ones, the Cheyenne and the Arapaho, stay mostly up in Wyoming and Dakota territory. Not that I trust any of them. I'm always very careful when I come up here," Cindy said. "But I didn't bring you here to talk about Indians, or anything else," she added, and her mouth came down hard on his. Her smallish body curled around him, legs drawn up to press into him, little dark triangle rubbing against him, exciting in its soft-fiber texture. "Oh, oooh, yes," Cindy murmured as her little Venus mound felt the hot, pulsating firmness of him. Her small-featured face with its crown of dark brown, short-cut hair had an animated prettiness that grew more animated as her excitement spiraled. Cindy's mouth opened on his, her tongue darting out, quick, short, fervent motions, and her small, almost thin body rubbed up and down his powerful frame.

Catlike, she rubbed against him, enjoying the feel of him, the touch of him against her, responding to the explosion of sensuality that was part of her. She rubbed and moved and clung and rubbed again, and he felt the excitement spiraling through himself, matching her half-giggly heat. He brought his mouth down to the so-soft breasts, felt their pink tips grow wet as he sucked on them, and she made sighing little sounds. The clock turned back, and once again he was holding himself inside her, immersing himself in the eager wanting of her, feeling the unfettered pleasure of her, and it was as if time had never passed. Cindy quivered as she clung, then half screamed as she enjoyed every erotic impulse and blanketed his body with hers, making use of passion to make up for her small size.

But, finally, as her cries dwindled away, she lay against him, her little half smile made of absolute satisfaction. She was still half wrapped around him when he heard the sound of hoofbeats approaching the cabin. They came to a halt, and a woman's voice called out, full of strain and tension. "Hello, inside the cabin. I need help. Anyone in there?" Fargo heard the sound of the rider dismounting, and he started to sit up as Cindy unwrapped her legs from around his. "Hello in there," the voice called again, this time accompanied by a fist pounding on the door. Fargo pushed to a sitting position as Cindy, one leg underneath her, also sat up. He was starting to reach for trousers when the door opened, and a young woman stepped into the cabin, her eyes widening at once. "Oh, my," she breathed as little spots of color appeared on smooth, flat cheeks. "I seem to have come at a bad time," she said, but looked more annoyed than dismayed.

"A bad time would've been a minute ago. Now you're just inconvenient," Fargo said, and the little spots of color widened. She was very attractive, dark blond hair pulled back in a bun, blue eyes with arching brows, prominent cheekbones, and a full figure inside a tightly buttoned dark brown dress. But she didn't hide her disapproval as she took in Cindy and himself with her lips pulled thin.

"I'm inconvenient, but there are three wagons of men, women, and children dead in an Indian attack. It's terrible. You've got to come," she said.

"Where?"

"In the valley, just south of here," she said.

"The attack still going on?" Fargo questioned.

"No."

"Then it's too late," Fargo said.

"I came onto the wagons and rode away to find help. I saw the cabin and stopped. There may be people still alive," she said.

"All right," Fargo said and saw her turn away as he started to stand up to dress.

"I'll be outside," she said, then hurried past the door. Fargo quickly pulled on clothes and shot a glance at Cindy. "Thought you said the tribes were peaceful around here," he reminded her.

"They have been," Cindy said.

"Get dressed. I don't want you staying on here alone," Fargo said.

"I'll be along. I know the valley. You go on with her," Cindy said, and Fargo hurried from the cabin to see the young woman astride a tall-legged bay gelding. Fargo swung onto the Ovaro and came alongside her as she led the way down a deer trail between stands of black oak.

"What brought you out here on your own?" Fargo asked.

"I was trying to catch up to the wagons," she said, and Fargo's brows lifted as he glanced at her. "I've three wagons in Dennison. I wanted to join up with Derek Hogath's wagons. He's the man heading the train. I wanted to catch up to them and see if they'd wait and let us join them."

"You were all going to the same place?" Fargo questioned.

"To the new fort," she said.

"Fort Sanders by the Black Hills up South Dakota way?" Fargo asked.

"That's the one. I want to be there for the dedication," she said and led the way down a sharp offshoot of the trail. "By the way, I'm Alison Carter."

"Skye Fargo."

The small valley came into sight, and Fargo rode onto the open land to see the three covered wagons a thousand feet ahead. But they were not the only sight that held his eyes. A line of blue-coated United States cavalry troopers was halted alongside the scene of the attack. "They came after I rode off for help," Alison Carter said. "I'd say they just got here." Fargo slowed and reined to a halt as he reached the troopers, where an officer had already dismounted and turned to him. Fargo saw a young face, blue eyes and light brown hair, a crisply pressed uniform on a slender, straight-backed body, lieutenant's bars on his shoulders.

"Maybe the young lady'd best stay back," the lieutenant said. Fargo saw that he was trying hard to keep his own face from showing shock.

"She was here before you. She came and brought me," Fargo said.

"Lieutenant Tom Bowdon, Troop C, U.S. Cavalry," the lieutenant said with the kind of formality that masked inexperience with earnestness and pain with stiffness.

"Skye Fargo. This is Alison Carter," Fargo said and swung down from the Ovaro, his eyes sweeping the scene. "Guess we were all too late."

"My God, what a terrible massacre," Lieutenant Bowdon muttered, shock in his voice.

"Your first one?" Fargo asked, and the young officer swallowed hard as he nodded. Fargo slowly walked among the still, slain bodies of the men, woman, and children, all with multiple arrows imbedded in them, even the children. His eyes also took in the personal belongings strewn and scattered all around the scene.

"Hostiles, of course," Lieutenant Bowdon said and touched the end of one of the arrows sticking up from a man's back. "I'm not that familiar with tribal decoration. I'll take a few arrows back to Major Elmont at the post. He'll know."

"Cheyenne," Fargo said and saw Bowdon glance quickly at him.

"You seem sure," the young officer said.

"I am. Been reading Indian signs for too long. Sometimes I'm called the Trailsman," Fargo said.

"You tell from the markings on the arrows?"

"That, the kind of arrows, and the way the arrowheads are wrapped onto the shafts. Different tribes have their own distinctive methods of wrapping their arrowheads and a liking for certain woods," Fargo said as his explanation was suddenly interrupted by a sound from the line

15

of box elder. Everyone spun at once, eyes on the dense trees, Fargo with the big Colt instantly out of its holster. The figure staggered out of the trees, stumbled, then almost fell, a middle-aged man with blood trickling down one side of his temple. The lieutenant barked orders, and three troopers rushed to the man, catching him before he fell. They eased him down against the rear wheel of one of the wagons.

"It's Hogath," the lieutenant said and stepped toward the man.

"Derek Hogath," Alison said at Fargo's shoulder. "He organizes wagon expeditions. He's the man I was coming to see."

Fargo moved closer to where the lieutenant was having one of his troopers apply a bandage to the man's head.

"They sprang out of the trees," Derek Hogath said. "I jumped from my wagon and was hit on the ground. They must have thought they'd killed me, but I somehow rolled into the trees. Anyone else survive?"

"No," Lieutenant Bowdon said.

"My God, my God," Derek Hogath moaned.

"You get a good look at them?" Bowdon asked.

"No, it all happened so fast. But they were Indians, all wearing war paint. I can't tell you what kind they were," Hogath said.

"Cheyenne, according to Mister Fargo, here," the lieutenant said.

"I didn't exactly say that," Fargo put in and drew a frown from the lieutenant. "I said they used Cheyenne arrows."

The lieutenant's frown deepened. "You saying they

were some other Indians using Cheyenne arrows?" he questioned.

Fargo didn't answer, but walked along the grisly scene, his lake blue eyes hardening as he scanned the ground, analyzing every mark, reading every sign, understanding the meaning of little things others saw only with passing glances. Finally, he turned back to the lieutenant. "I'm saying this wasn't an Indian attack," Fargo said and heard the small gasp from the others.

"You serious?" Bowdon asked.

"Real serious. A lot of things don't hang together," Fargo said.

"But Mister Hogath saw Indians; you heard him. Indians wearing war paint," the lieutenant said.

"That's one of the things," Fargo said. "The Cheyenne wouldn't put on war paint to attack a few wagons. Indians put on war paint when they signify they're gone to war in a major way or when they go into a really important battle. He saw men made up as Indians in case they were seen running away or if there were survivors still able to talk."

"I looked at the hoofprints. They're unshod. Look at them yourself. That means Indian pony prints," Bowdon said.

"Usually, but not this time. They were real clever. I looked at the prints," Fargo said and pointed to a spot some twenty yards on. "Look at where they galloped away. The strides are much too long for short-legged Indian ponies. These were made by big horses with their shoes removed."

The lieutenant's frown stayed. "The Cheyenne arrows?"

"Collected from one or another place. That wouldn't

17

be hard to do," Fargo said and gestured to the lifeless forms strewn beside the wagons. "The arrows are another thing that doesn't fit. There are three to six arrows in every body, including children. The Indian never wastes arrows. Arrows are too precious. They take a lot of time and work to make. The Indian never uses three when one will do. The Cheyenne never put all those arrows in these people." He paused as the lieutenant took in the scene with his young, earnest face growing grave. "There's more," Fargo said. "All these personal belongings scattered around. Indians take trophies, clothes, jewelry, weapons, blankets, whatever takes their fancy. Then they burn the wagons. That's the Indian way. These wagons were emptied and everything searched through and then left, and that's not the Indian way of attacking a wagon train."

Lieutenant Bowdon regarded Fargo with earnest seriousness. "Very impressive," he murmured.

"Very," Derek Hogath added. "But if you're right, what does it mean? What were they looking for? Why did they have to kill everybody?"

"I can take a guess at the last question. They killed everybody because they didn't know who had whatever they wanted," Fargo said.

"And we don't know if they found whatever they were after," Hogath said.

"That's right," Fargo said and spun around with the others at the sound of a horse from behind. Cindy appeared from around the box elder, and Fargo spoke out quickly. "She's with me," he said, and Cindy rode to a halt, glanced at the scene, then looked away.

"I'll send a burial detail from the post," the lieutenant said.

"Can you have your men bring the wagons back?" Derek Hogath asked. "No sense in wasting perfectly good wagons."

"I'll do that. You can ride one of our mounts," Bowdon said, and one of the troopers brought his horse over. Fargo swung onto the Ovaro as Cindy came alongside him. He waited and let the lieutenant place his troops in front and behind the three wagons as they started to move back across the valley.

"You still pulling out in a few days?" Cindy asked Fargo.

"Figure to," Fargo said.

"I don't feel much like going back to the cabin. There's a good cot in the back room of the store. Pa goes to bed early," she said.

"We'll talk on it," he said and put the Ovaro into a slow trot as the lieutenant set his troops forward at a good pace. Alison Carter rode beside Hogath, he noted, and the procession was nearing Dennison and the army post when Hogath turned his horse and rode back to Fargo. Alison Carter followed and drew up alongside.

"Alison told me they call you the Trailsman. From the way you read things back there, you're very good," Derek Hogath said. "I'd like to hire you to take us through."

"Us?" Fargo queried.

"I've three more wagons waiting, and Miss Carter wants to join. She'll pay half your fee. We want to get through this time, and we're both very concerned. We don't know if whoever attacked those wagons found what they were looking for. If they didn't, they might attack again," Hogath said.

"That's right." Fargo nodded. "You've no idea what they were after?"

"None whatsoever," Derek Hogath said.

"Why are you running these wagon trains to Fort Sanders? It's not even dedicated yet," Fargo said.

"I'm bringing good families who want to establish a community and be safe. Most of the main forts have established communities around them. That's how towns are built out here, by families who spread out and put down roots. Even command posts have towns that grew up around them such as Dennison. Both the communities and the army benefit."

"Besides, Fort Sanders is going to be in operation very soon, in about a week, I understand, with an initial complement of troops with more to come in time," Alison said. "In fact, Major Foster at the Dennison Command Post is to be the first commander of Fort Sanders."

Fargo took a moment to peer at Alison Carter's contained, dark blond attractiveness that she kept guarded with a slightly starchy manner. "You going to set down roots outside the new fort?" he asked.

"In a way," she said. He smiled inwardly. It was a less than direct answer, but he decided not to press further as Derek Hogath broke into his thoughts.

"I hope you'll agree to take us, Fargo. I'll need an answer by the morning," the man said.

"We'll need an answer," Alison corrected, and Fargo nodded as he sent the pinto forward, the houses of Dennison looming up ahead and beyond them, the buildings of the army command post spread in a loose square surrounded by a stockade. Cindy caught up to him and rode at his side until they reached the sprawling buildings of Dennison, a community that had over the years become a town that boasted a bank as well as a saloon. It was still, however, not much of a town, with at least half its citizens tending small farms that stretched miles beyond the town area. Yet as Cindy had said, the Indian tribes in the area had stayed peaceful. But that wouldn't be so at the Black Hills in Dakota territory. The real Cheyenne roamed that land. Settlers would need a full-size fort.

"You come visiting tonight?" Cindy asked, breaking into his musings. "After nine."

"Count on it," Fargo said, and she turned her horse away to ride down a side street toward her pa's general store. Fargo rode on to the open gates of the stockade and waited to one side as the lieutenant led his troops into the post. Alison Carter turned away, and Fargo watched her ride to the far end of the town main street, where she dismounted beside three wagons, each a Texas wagon outfitted with top bows and a canvas cover. She disappeared into one of the wagons as Lieutenant Bowdon came over to him.

"I'm going to report to Major Foster. I'd like you to be there, Fargo," Bowdon said.

"No problem," Fargo said, dismounted, and followed the lieutenant into a square, flat-roofed building separated from the long barracks buildings and the stables. He entered an office where the man behind the desk rose, and Fargo saw a smallish-figured man in a sharply pressed uniform.

"Major Foster," the lieutenant introduced. "This here is Mister Skye Fargo," he said to the major.

"Major Elmont Foster," the officer said with a curt nod and came around to the front of the desk. He moved with quick steps, a slightly bantam rooster air to him, and Fargo took in a sharp nose, black hair, and a pencil-thin mustache that seemed almost stenciled on a short upper lip.

"We ran into serious trouble on patrol. Fargo was present, and I wanted him to be here during my report," the lieutenant said and launched into a crisp, concise report in which he outlined in detail everything Fargo had said. When he finished, Major Foster pursed his lips for a long moment.

"Thank you, Lieutenant Bowdon," the major said finally. "Please attend to the burial detail while I talk with Mister Fargo."

"Yes, sir," Bowdon said and hurried from the room. The major offered Fargo a condescending smile that was not echoed in his eyes.

"Tell me, Mister Fargo, did you enjoy confusing my young lieutenant?" the major asked.

Fargo's eyes narrowed. "I thought I was helping him see the truth of it," he said evenly. "I take it you don't agree with that."

"You came up with a crock of shit," the major snapped. Fargo fought back a quick answer. He'd take a little more time to take the measure of Major Elmont Foster. Right now, he could only wrestle with his own surprise.

2

"Strong words, Major," Fargo said.

"Entirely warranted," Major Foster replied, his tone retaining its condescension. "You've chosen to indulge in wild interpretation. For example, this wouldn't be the first time the Cheyenne have come down this far to attack."

"When was the last time you saw them?" Fargo interrupted.

"My predecessor mentioned it to me," the major said. "As to the long strides of the horses, it's obvious they rode captured horses."

"The Cheyenne wouldn't ride captured horses all the way down here. They'd use the ponies they're at home with. They use captured horses near home to pull travois and more often than not as horse meat."

"The reason they didn't burn the wagons was no doubt because they heard Troop C approaching," the major said, ignoring his answer to the previous statement. "They didn't stop to take anything for the same reason. All your other points are highly disputable, also. Really, why would anyone other than Indians attack three wagons?"

"You've got me there. Damned if I know," Fargo said.

"But you still hold to your quaint interpretations?"

"I always hold to what I know is right. I'm funny that way," Fargo said, and Major Foster didn't bother to put on his condescending smile.

"Good day, Fargo," he said curtly. Fargo tossed him a nod as he walked from the office. Outside, he led the Ovaro by the reins and came upon Lieutenant Bowdon returning to the major's quarters.

"You have a good meeting with Major Foster?" Bowdon asked.

"I wouldn't exactly put it that way," Fargo muttered. "The major didn't agree with anything I said. He had a different read on everything. I'm sure he'll tell you."

The lieutenant's frown was part surprise and part apology. "Sorry, sir. Guess the major thinks I'm easy to convince," he said uncomfortably.

"Do you think you are?" Fargo smiled.

"I don't think so, but then I don't really know a hell of a lot," Bowdon said honestly.

"Neither does the major. He's a pompous little ass who likes to hear himself talk," Fargo snapped.

Fargo saw the lieutenant stiffen at once. "He's my commanding officer. I'll thank you to respect him," Bowdon said.

"Sorry. Of course," Fargo apologized and kept a smile within himself as he walked on. He understood Bowdon's young earnestness and loyalties. The army demanded loyalty. Obedience, discipline, and loyalty were its cornerstones, and he respected that. It was both right and understandable. But he also knew the other aspects of the army. It was an organization captured by its own structure, a hiding place for mediocrity, a refuge for men such as Major Foster. But it also nurtured great leaders such as his old friend Miles Stanford. As he walked on, Fargo saw that the major had come outside and was giving the lieutenant his version of things, no doubt accompanied by a warning against listening to civilians. The major could be seen as harmless, yet the man's brand of bantam rooster arrogance all too often masked dangerousness. Incompetence and authority were usually a bad combination.

But if the major could be seen as an eminently dismissable figure, the attack could not, Fargo pondered. Had it accomplished its purpose, or would there be another in perhaps another disguise? The question hung unanswered, just like his decision whether to take the wagons or not, he realized, and he shifted direction as he spied Alison Carter pulling down the tailgate of one of the Texas bow wagons. She turned as he came up, the Ovaro at his heels. "That is a magnificent horse," she said. "Didn't have a chance to mention that before." He nodded agreement and stroked the handsome black forequarters that contrasted with the glistening white midsection and jet hindquarters. "Have you come to tell us you'll take us on?" Alison asked.

"Not yet. Maybe you better talk to Major Foster. He didn't agree with anything I said," Fargo told her.

"I'd hardly pay attention to him." Alison Carter sniffed. "I've met him twice and didn't care for him."

"The army thinks enough of him to give him command of their newest fort," Fargo said.

"The army does a lot of things that should be undone," Alison said, crinkling her nose.

"A personal beef?" Fargo queried.

"Just observation," she said, and he was studying Alison Carter's controlled attractiveness when the canvas

25

went up on two of the other wagons, and Fargo saw three young women step out.

"Hello," the first one said in a husky voice, and Fargo took in a woman in her mid-twenties, he guessed, a wide face pleasant more than pretty, medium brown hair and brown eyes, a slightly pudgy face followed by a figure a little overblown, just edging heaviness. Yet she radiated a friendly, open air. "I'm Brenda Jackson," she said.

"Pearl Smith," the woman beside her said and gazed out of very round, dark brown eyes. She was a little older than Brenda Jackson, but she had the same open friendliness. Her body was very different, thin, almost sticklike with small breasts barely pushing out from a cotton shirt. Fargo's eyes went to the third young woman, about the same age as the others, but she stood very straight, an air of quiet reserve to her. Thick black hair surrounded a handsome, somewhat angular face with prominent cheekbones, black eyes, and a faintly copper hue to her skin.

"Ida Bluebell," she said, not unfriendly at all, yet without the smiles the others had given. A straight dress hid most of her shape, and Fargo turned to Alison Carter. She was much the same age as the other three women, he noted.

"These ladies the rest of your group?" he asked.

"Yes," Alison said. "Anything wrong with that?" she added, a cool edge to her voice.

A furrow dug itself into Fargo's brow. "What kind of roots you figure on setting down?" he asked.

"These ladies are all trained midwives," Alison said. "A new community is going to need midwives. God knows when they'll be getting a doctor."

The furrow deepened in Fargo's brow. "Midwives?

Aren't you rushing it, honey? I don't see that there'll be any need for even one midwife much less three, no matter how much screwing is done."

She tossed him a disapproving glance. "I believe in being prepared," she said stiffly.

"Where do you fit in? You going to be den mother?" he questioned.

"I'm a nurse. I trained Brenda, Pearl, and Ida. I've come along to supervise them until they're ready to be on their own," Alison said, and Fargo's eyes stayed on her. Her explanations didn't satisfy. New families would have a lot to do before adding children. There'd be no need for midwives for nine months to a year at the earliest. "I'm sorry you don't believe me," Alison said, reading the skepticism in his face. "Go on, say what you're thinking," she challenged.

He returned a wry smile. "You blame me? Fancy girls settle into new communities, specially with the army as a neighbor."

"Do I look like a madam?" Alison asked sharply.

"No, that's for sure," Fargo said.

"Then I'll thank you for an apology," she said and sniffed.

"It's yours. How could I have been so wrong?" he said blandly and saw the three young women smiling brightly at him.

"I hope you'll be taking us," Brenda Jackson said.

"I'll sleep on it," Fargo said and walked on as dusk began to lower across the little collection of buildings they called a town. Maybe he'd been wrong in thinking they might be fancy girls, but he didn't accept Alison's story. It didn't hang right, but he was intrigued by it, he admitted and set it aside for the moment. Dusk had turned into night when he stopped at the saloon, as small and dingy as Dennison itself. But they served a decent buffalo sandwich, and when he'd finished eating, he went to Cindy to find her waiting outside.

"Pa decided to work late," she said. "He wants my help. Let's try for tomorrow night."

"If I'm here," Fargo said.

"You going to take the wagons out?" she asked.

"I'm thinking about it. I'm free till next month. Hate to turn down good money," he said, and she nodded. There was more, he admitted to himself. Three wagons of men, women, and children had been savagely slain. Their deaths deserved a reason, a justification and proper blame. Then there was the possibility that the attack could be repeated, and that stuck inside him. And Alison Carter's story, though but a sidelight, continued to intrigue him.

He was still turning his thoughts over when he saw the major standing outside the stockade near a lantern beside a thin, reedy figure dressed in army-issue boots but wearing an Indian shawl and tattered britches. The man's long, straight black hair, broad, heavily cheekboned face, and brow band marked him as all or mostly Indian. "Mister Fargo," Major Foster called out. "This is Thin Tree, one of my regular scouts. He's Cheyenne. I was telling him about your quaint interpretation of that wagon raid."

"He agreed with you, of course," Fargo said.

"Of course." The major smiled in his arrogantly condescending way. "In fact, he tells me he's been hearing about an increasing Cheyenne presence down this far."

"Is that so," Fargo said. The major's eyes narrowed slightly, but he held onto his smile.

"Why do I have the feeling you're going to stick to your version?" he said.

"Because you've got to be right once in a while," Fargo said and had the pleasure of seeing the condescending smile fade. He looked at the scout, holding his gaze on the man's dark, impassive face. He was fairly conversant in Algonkian, the tongue spoken by the Cheyenne as well as the Blackfoot, Arapaho, and the Plains Ojibway. "The major is stupid. You are a liar," Fargo said in Algonkian to the scout. The man made no reply, and his face remained thoroughly unchanged as Fargo walked on. Fargo strode beyond the stockade and was about to swing onto the Ovaro when he saw Alison's three wagons and a figure come from the last one toward him. He halted as Brenda Jackson materialized, clad in a loose cotton nightdress that reached to her ankles in billowy shapelessness, only her sizable breasts taking form.

"Going to bed down?" she asked, and he nodded. "Where?" she followed.

"Just past town. There's a small hillside of hawthorne," Fargo said.

"Sleep well," she said, her face blandly pleasant. He climbed onto the horse and felt her eyes watching him as he rode on. Passing the last buildings of Dennison, he saw the small hill and made his way to the cluster of hawthorns at the top. The night stayed warm, and he set down his bedroll, then undressed to his underdrawers and stretched out under a half-moon. He waited, a slight smile on his lips, and it wasn't long before he heard the sound, the soft tread of a horse moving slowly. He sat up, not bothering to put his hand on the Colt alongside him.

"Over here," he said as he saw the rider appear. The horse was being ridden without a saddle he noted as Brenda Jackson slid to the ground. She halted and let her eyes move across the smoothness of his muscled body, finally halting at his face. "I expected you'd be surprised," she said with a half smile.

"You expected wrong," Fargo said.

She gave a wry shrug. "Should've known better," she said.

"You want to tell me why you're here?" Fargo asked.

"Yes. I wouldn't want you to get the wrong idea," Brenda Jackson said.

"You come on your own, or did you draw straws?" Fargo queried.

"On my own. Alison would have a cat fit if she knew I was here," Brenda said and sank to her knees on the bedroll.

"You're going behind her back," Fargo said.

"Not the way you make it sound. Alison's a very remarkable person. We owe her a lot. We wouldn't be here without her. I wouldn't go behind her back to hurt her. I know this might make you wonder again if we're fancy girls," Brenda said.

"Bull's-eye," Fargo agreed.

"We're not, none of us. But I worked as a dance hall waitress for a couple of years. I know more about how to change a man's mind than the others do. I came because I want you to help Alison, to help all of us. I came to do whatever it takes to get you to do that."

"That's plain talk," Fargo said.

"Guess it is," Brenda Jackson said, her slightly pudgy face growing very serious.

"I'll give you plain talk back. It won't make any difference, honey," Fargo said.

Brenda's lips tightened as she stared at him, and she finally offered a shrug and a sigh. "I was afraid of that. I was afraid you'd be different," she murmured.

"Sorry about that," Fargo said. "You can say good night, now."

Brenda's eyes moved slowly across his near naked body, and her gaze returned to his lake blue eyes. "What if I said I'd stay?" she asked. "It's been a long, dry past, and God knows what the future holds. It's plain you're something special, and I'm here. I can't see any bad out of making the most of it."

"I can't, either, now that you put it that way," Fargo said, and Brenda flashed a quick smile as she reached her arms up and whisked the nightdress over her head, then tossed it aside. Fargo's eyes moved over a body that just avoided being heavy, a full-fleshed body with a few extra folds at the waist, yet with no flabbiness to her. Almost pendulous breasts kept their shape, each tipped with a large, dark pink areola and a prominent nipple already standing firm. Another small fold topped a round belly, and below it, a surprisingly modest triangle, and then full-thighed legs with sturdy calves. Brenda reached out for him, and he lay back and pulled her with him. She pressed the large breasts into his abdomen, and he enjoyed their softness.

She ran her hand across his muscled smoothness, and he heard her little half cry of delight. He turned, took her with him, and closed his mouth around one large breast, pulling it deep and feeling the soft pillowiness of it. "Aaaah," Brenda cried out. "Ah, yes, ah, yes." He sucked on it, caressed its fullness with his tongue, and his hand explored across the well-covered rib cage, across the soft bulge of her belly, over the dip that went down to the moist triangle. "Oh, oh, Jeeeez . . ." Brenda gasped, and he felt full-fleshed thighs fall open and her ample torso half twisted. He reached down farther, closing his hand around the waiting opening, and she closed her thighs over his hand, and he felt the moistness of her. She held him for a moment, and then the full thighs fell open, releasing their soft grip, and Brenda gave a guttural sound as he touched deeper.

He brought himself to her after a moment as he felt the urgency of her. Tiny breaths and quick half words implored, the body making its own language, and her fingers were digging into his buttocks as he slipped his pulsating warmth into her. "Oh, Jeeeez," Brenda cried out as she pushed upward, the first of a series of long, surging thrusts, each one accompanied by a guttural sound of pure, erotic pleasure. The almost pendulous breasts rose and fell with her every movement, slipped to one side, then the other, returned to push against him, and he buried his face in their very soft fullness. Brenda's arms were around his neck, her full-fleshed thighs around his hips as she surged against him, and the deep, guttural cries grew deeper and stronger until finally, with a shuddering scream that somehow stayed half inside her, her moment exploded, and he let himself go with her. "Arrrgh, arrrgh . . . God, God, ah, ah, ah, yes," Brenda cried out against him, enveloping him with her softness, enfolding him with her hot flesh, encompassing them both with her pure pleasure that brought unique wonder in its simple, sensory exuberance.

When finally her thighs fell open and her surging body lay still, her warm, round belly against him, breasts partly flattened into his chest, she uttered tiny, satisfied sounds and was asleep in his arms almost at once. He drew away from her, and she gave only a small sigh with her eyes closed, and when he lay beside her, she turned so one breast rested against his chest. Sound asleep, she stayed that way, and he finally closed his eyes and slept.

It was dawn when he opened his eyes, half rose, and shook her. "Shouldn't you be back at the wagon?" he asked, and Brenda Jackson's eyes snapped awake.

"Oh, God, yes," she said, springing up, breasts swinging as she threw on the nightdress. He rose and helped her onto the horse. "I'm glad I came," she said. "No matter what you decide."

"And you'll be going on, no matter what I decide," he said, and she nodded. "You're very stubborn, all of you," he said.

"Determined," she said. "There's a difference."

"Determined is for people with a mission," he said.

"Being a midwife's a mission," she said as she rode away, and he watched her until she was out of sight. He smiled as he lay down on the bedroll. The answer had been almost glib, yet he couldn't dismiss it entirely, even though the reason still didn't sit right with him. He let himself doze until the sun came over the mountains and then used his canteen to wash. When he'd finished dressing, he leisurely rode to Dennison, had coffee at the saloon, and walked on, the Ovaro following. He had just reached Alison's three wagons when she stepped from one and strode toward him. He saw the tension in her face as she halted before him, her eyes searching his.

"You have anything to say?" Alison asked.

"About what?" he inquired, one brow lifting.

"Brenda. I was up when she came in," Alison said.

"Nothing more than she did," Fargo said carefully.

"She said she couldn't sleep and went for a ride. She said you were up."

Fargo couldn't stop the fleeting smile that crossed his face. "I sure was," he said blandly.

"She's very vulnerable. We all are. I hope you didn't take advantage of her," Alison said severely.

"Me?"

She fixed a disapproving stare on him. "From what I saw at that cabin, you have no hesitation indulging yourself," she said, reproach in her tone.

"None at all," Fargo agreed cheerfully, and she continued to look disapprovingly at him as he walked on to where Derek Hogath talked to a cluster of men, women, and children. Hogath wore a fresh patch on his square face, and Fargo noted an air of courtliness to the man he hadn't caught before.

"Morning, Fargo," Derek said with a bow of his head. "Been going over things with these good people. I hope you have the answer we all want to hear."

"What happens if I say no?" Fargo questioned.

Derek Hogath's face seemed to sag. "We'd be mighty disappointed," he said.

"What else? Would you call off going?" Fargo pressed.

"Call it off? No, we wouldn't do that. There's no telling how long we'd have to wait. We'll just take our chances and go on. We'll hope for the best and say our prayers," the man answered, more sadness than anger in his voice.

"All right, you win. I'll take you," Fargo said, and the shout of approval was led by Derek Hogath.

"Hallelujah," Hogath said. "Now, I'll finish listing the basics I insist every family bring."

"Make a good rifle one of them," Fargo said.

"You expect there'll be another attack?" Hogath frowned.

"Can't say I expect so, but I want to be ready if there is," Fargo said.

"We ought to be ready to roll by noon tomorrow," Hogath called as Fargo walked on. He paused at a watering trough to let the Ovaro drink and found Alison there.

"I'll pay Derek Hogath my half of your fee and let him settle up with you," she said.

"Fine," Fargo said and saw Alison's eyes searching his face.

"Does this mean you've stopped being cynical about me . . . about what we're doing?" she asked.

"No," he said, but softened the answer with a smile. "I've a built-in cynical streak," he added.

Her chin lifted, a touch of defiance added to disapproval. "I feel sorry for you." She sniffed. "Going through life distrusting people must be very depressing."

"Especially when I'm right so often," Fargo said and swung onto the pinto as exasperation stayed in her glare. He rode from the sparseness of the town and headed north into the low hills where his eyes searched the terrain. He stayed in a clump of red ash as six Indians passed near, plainly a hunting party that had a white-tail slung over the back of one pony. Probably Ponca, he muttered, though he saw no markings he could recognize. He went on crossing the hill country and came onto various things in the grass, bushes, and trees, and near a pond, part of a choker, broken arrow shafts, an armband, the top of a moccasin, but nothing that bore Cheyenne markings.

When he finally made his way back, the day was beginning to draw to a close, and he was satisfied it hadn't been the Cheyenne who'd wiped out the wagons. Alison's wagons were grouped in a half circle with Derek Hogath's as he rode into town, and Hogath moved among the people. Fargo slowed as he spotted Major Foster walking toward him, Lieutenant Bowdon at his side, the Indian scout close behind. "Been waiting for you, Fargo," the major said. Fargo dismounted and included the lieutenant in his nod. "I hear you're going to take Derek Hogath's wagons out," the major said.

"Word gets around fast," Fargo said.

"This is a small community. Besides, Hogath's been telling everyone. I'm sure it's common news by now," the major said. "In addition, Hogath asked me if we might provide a military escort at least part of the way."

"What was your answer?" Fargo asked.

"I told him that it was against army policy to provide escorts for private wagon trains. We'd be deluged with such requests if we did."

"This is a little different. There's been an attack. He's concerned because of that," Fargo said.

"I am, too. That's why I've been waiting for you. I'd prefer you didn't take the wagons to Fort Sanders at this time," Foster said, and Fargo's brows lifted. "Despite your wild interpretation of signs, it's obvious the Cheyenne are down here raiding. I can't commit the necessary troops to hunt them down. That leaves the wagons at a particular risk."

"Not if you send a patrol along part of the way, at least," Fargo said.

"Impossible. I have to keep enough men here to escort a very important party of officials to Fort Sanders for the dedication. I must also use most of my men to establish a garrison at the fort. I'm sure you've heard that I'll be commanding Fort Sanders," the major said.

"I heard. Who's in the official party?" Fargo queried.

"Senator Connolly representing the President. Herbert Matso, secretary of the army. Senators Williams and Drew of the Military Affairs Committee, General Hawkins, army chief of staff, and other dignitaries. I've a complete list in my office. In addition, my orders are to keep the dedication simple. I want to discourage outside attendance. I'd rather these settlers arrive at the fort after the dignitaries have left. So you see there are numerous reasons for you not to take the wagons."

"Except one. They're going to go whether I take them or not," Fargo said.

"I think they may not," the major said loftily.

"You're wrong, again," Fargo grunted, and the major's eyes narrowed.

"So you're going to help them be stupid," the major tossed at him.

"I hope I'll help them stay alive," Fargo said.

"I'll remember your cooperation," Major Foster said as he strode away. The lieutenant followed him, but gave Fargo an apologetic shrug. Fargo moved forward, the pinto following, and paused at the half circle of wagons as night began to close down.

"We'll be ready come morning," Derek Hogath said, his voice filled with eager enthusiasm. "I've a good feeling about everything with you along, Fargo."

"Hope you're right," Fargo said and silently wished he could summon up the man's optimism. As he walked on, Pearl Smith emerged from one of the wagons, a tan shirt resting on her shallow breasts and somehow giving them a slender provocativeness. Her round, dark eyes seemed to dance with dark fire.

"Hello," she said, her voice softly husky. "Going to spend the night here with us?"

"Not likely. I'm used to being off by myself," Fargo said.

"Going back to the hawthorns where you were last night?" Pearl Smith asked.

"How do you know where I was last night?" Fargo returned with quiet amusement.

"Brenda told me," the young woman said, a slight smile touching her lips.

"What else did she tell you?" Fargo asked.

"Just girl talk," a voice broke in, and Fargo saw Brenda swing down from the wagon, her smile sly.

"That could cover a lot," Fargo said evenly.

"We share a lot," another voice broke in, and Ida Bluebell stepped out from behind the wagon, unsmiling, her quiet, tight body standing very straight, her handsome, coppery-hued face edging impassiveness. "It's worked out that way," she added.

"That include Alison?" Fargo asked. The three young women, each very different from the others, exchanged quick glances.

"Alison's different. She's our leader. She's with us and yet apart from us," Pearl Smith answered.

"Do the mice confide in the cat?" Brenda giggled, and Fargo saw Alison approaching with a bucket of water.

"Here comes the cat," he said, and the three young women fell silent as Alison put down the bucket. Fargo saw her take in everyone with a quick glance that told him she was both very sharp and very perceptive.

"Am I interrupting something?" she questioned.

"We were just asking if Fargo was going to bed down here with us," Brenda said.

"He told us he prefers being alone," Pearl said.

"Not exactly accurate," Alison said with an edge of tartness in her glance at Fargo. "He prefers cabins tucked away."

Fargo chuckled as the three young women turned their eyes to him. "If I'm not interrupted," he said and saw Alison's cheeks color. "See you tomorrow, ladies," he said and walked on.

Night had descended, and he slowly made his way to the saloon where he ate and toyed with a bourbon before leaving to go to Cindy's place. He was just about to swing up onto the pinto when a figure stepped from the darker shadows. Fargo's hand went to the Colt at his hip as the man came closer. "That's close enough," Fargo said.

"Want to talk," the man said, and Fargo kept his hand on the gun.

"Another three steps," he said, and the man came closer, becoming a medium-height figure with straggly black hair and a thin nose. "Who are you?" Fargo asked.

"Buddy," the man said. "You're the trailsman taking the wagons, right?"

"Might be," Fargo said.

"They said you rode a big Ovaro," the man said. "Somebody wants to see you."

"Who?"

"Somebody with something to sell you."

"Such as?"

"Information."

"What kind of information?" Fargo queried.

"About that wagon attack," the man said, and Fargo

felt excitement spiral inside him. "He'll tell you. I'm just the messenger," the man said.

"Where do I find him, Buddy?" Fargo questioned.

"I'll take you," Buddy said.

Fargo let thoughts tumble through his mind. He could be sucked into a trap, yet no one had reason to do that. He didn't see himself as important enough. Then there were always the sharpies who'd try to turn rumor into a chance for an extra dollar. They'd invent information to sell. Fargo was confident he could see through that. On the other hand, if someone did have information, it was too important to pass up. "Get your horse, Buddy," he said softly and swung onto the Ovaro as the man disappeared into the black shadows to emerge on a gray mare. "I'll be riding behind you," Fargo said, and the man shrugged as he turned his horse. Fargo swung in directly behind and followed as the man rode out of Dennison. Buddy said he was just a messenger. He didn't know it, but he was also going to be a shield, Fargo thought.

3

Buddy led the way from Dennison into thickly forested land, used deer trails through red ash, and box elder. Fargo rode with one hand on the reins, the other on the Colt at his hip. He peered into the night, his ears tuned for every sound, and Buddy finally turned from the deer trail to nose through the red ash. Suddenly, the tree line ended and a patch of open land appeared, bathed in the pale light of a half-moon. Buddy halted only a few dozen feet from the thick tree line, and Fargo's voice stayed soft as he bit out commands. "Get off your horse, nice and slow," Fargo ordered. The man obeyed, and Fargo swung from the Ovaro at the same time. He had the Colt pressed into the man's back instantly. "Don't move," he said, staying close against the man.

"Easy, easy," Buddy said nervously.

"I'm the man you want to see," a voice said, and Fargo saw a figure step from the trees, a medium-height man with dark, straggly hair and a pinched face. "I've got the information you want," he said.

"You've got a name?" Fargo questioned.

"Joe," the man said.

"How about the rest of it?"

"That'll do," the man said.

"Drop your gun, Joe," Fargo said. "It'd make me feel better." The man hesitated. "I'm nervous, and you don't want Buddy to get hurt, do you? Good messengers are hard to come by." The man lifted his six-gun from its holster, bent down, and placed it on the ground. Fargo stayed tight against Buddy as he kept the Colt pressed into the man's back. "Talk, Joe," he said.

"I want five hundred dollars," Joe said.

"That's a lot of money," Fargo said.

"It's worth what I can tell you," Joe said.

"If that's so, the money's yours. You've my word on it," Fargo said.

"The Cheyenne didn't raid those wagons," Joe said.

"Tell me something I don't know," Fargo said.

"I can't talk with Buddy standing between us. Get away from him," the man said.

"And be a clear target? No, thanks," Fargo said.

"My gun's on the ground," Joe said.

"Your gun," Fargo said. "Maybe you've got friends. I'll stay right here. Buddy makes a good shield."

"Not anymore," the man said and gestured with one hand.

"No, Jesus—" Buddy screamed, but his words were cut short as the five shots exploded from inside the trees. Fargo shuddered as the bullets smashed into Buddy, who seemed to gyrate in place before he crumpled to the ground. Fargo cursed silently as he stood completely exposed, a helpless target.

"Christ, he was your own man," Fargo accused.

"I'm real sorry about that," Joe said, but didn't sound sorry at all. "I'll take your gun now." Fargo saw three figures step from the trees, each with gun in hand. His shield a lifeless form crumpled on the ground, Fargo let the Colt drop from his fingers. "Kick it over here," Joe said, and Fargo obeyed.

"Why?" he asked as the man picked up the gun and his own.

"Just doin' a job," Joe said.

Killers for hire, Fargo grunted inwardly. Ruthless, vicious killers icily willing to cut down one of their own. That made him less than optimistic about his own chances. "You ever have anything to tell me about the attack on the wagons?" he asked.

"Not really," the man said.

"You know anything about it?"

"No."

"You know why the wagons were attacked?" Fargo asked.

"No," the man said.

"You know who's behind it?"

"No."

"You don't know much, do you?"

"I know you're a dead man," Joe said, and one of the others uttered a harsh laugh. "But not here. Our orders are to make it someplace you won't be found if they come searching." One of the others moved into the trees and returned leading four horses while everyone else kept guns trained on Fargo. Joe swung onto one of the horses and gestured to Fargo. "Mount up," he growled, and Fargo pulled himself onto the Ovaro. The other three men took their mounts and surrounded him at once, one on each side of him and one behind. Joe led the way as they moved forward.

"Who hired you?" Fargo asked.

Joe hesitated a moment before answering. "Why not? You won't be telling anybody. Man named Kosta," he answered as he led the way across the open stretch of land.

"Who's Kosta?" Fargo queried.

"He hired us. That's all I know."

"Why me?" Fargo continued. "They'll go on without me."

"They won't get through without you. They might with you taking them. Somebody doesn't want to take that chance," Joe said.

"I'm flattered," Fargo grunted.

"What's so goddamn important about the wagons getting through?" Fargo wondered aloud.

"I don't know, and you're never going to find out," the answer came as the man led the way along a stand of staghorn sumac. Fargo cast a glance at the men on either side of him. They rode with easy confidence, and Fargo's thoughts raced. The razor-sharp, double-edged, slender throwing knife nestled inside the calf-holster around his leg. He'd have but one chance to use it, and he'd have to make it the right one. He sat relaxed on the Ovaro, waiting as few men knew how to wait, refusing to let fear corrode alertness, using danger to sharpen his every sense. They rode perhaps a half hour when he was led down an incline, and he saw a lake appear, sparkling quietly in the moonlight.

They halted close to the water, and as they did, Fargo's body tensed, and his right hand stole down to his calf. His hand seemed to merely brush against his trouser leg, a casual movement, but his fingers crept upward and lifted the slender blade from its sheath. He waited a moment longer and let Joe start to dismount. Their plan was obvious. They'd use rocks and rope to send him to the bottom of the lake. His powerful calf and thigh muscles tightening, Fargo yanked the slender blade from inside his trouser leg as he flung himself sideways from the saddle, all in one explosion of motion. He slammed into the rider at his left, and the man flew sideways out of his saddle as Fargo went with him. He hit the ground half atop the man and heard the shouts of alarm from the others. With a lightninglike sweep of his arm, the double-edged blade slicing in a flat arc, he did away with one would-be killer and a split second later dove into the lake before the others could get a shot off.

He was already underwater when shots rang out, and he heard the bullets smack into the water. But they were firing too quickly, their shots wild and, keeping underwater, he swam to his right and stayed in the shallowness close to the shore. He could hear the shots still being fired, a wildly erratic hail of bullets as he touched the soft bottom with both feet. Planting his feet into the lake bottom to gain balance and leverage, he rose and broke through the surface of the water with his right arm already raised to throw.

The three figures started to wheel their horses at the sound of his surfacing, but the slender blade was already hurtling through the night. The nearest of the three riders suddenly clutched at the base of his neck, emitted a hoarse, strangled sound, and toppled from his horse to land facedown almost in the water. Joe and the remaining figure were firing furiously now, but Fargo had already dived under the surface of the lake. Once again he swam underwater, this time striking out for the deeper water. He surfaced when his breath gave out and found himself almost at the center of the small lake. "There he is," he heard Joe yell and saw the two men at the shore.

A shot followed and skimmed over the water far off mark, and Fargo began to swim, staying above water. "Son of a bitch, he's going to the other side," a voice called out. Glancing shoreward, Fargo saw the two men spur their horses forward to race around the edge of the lake, but he kept swimming, long, unhurried strokes. The two riders reached the other side of the lake just as he drew closer to the shore, and he sank beneath the surface before they fired their first shot.

He swam underwater again until his lungs burned, and this time when he surfaced he was closer to the back section of the lake. "Goddammit, there he is," Joe shouted. Fargo stayed, treading water for a moment, and as the two horsemen raced to reach the shoreline before he did, he sank down again. Once more he swam underwater, reversing direction, and this time when he surfaced, he was near the shoreline at the top of the lake. Again it took a moment before the two men spotted him, but when they did, Joe's voice shouted at once. "Over there, goddamn him," he said, and Fargo saw both horses leap forward as the riders began to race around the lake shore to reach him. But Fargo measured the distance to the shore, decided he was close enough to reach it, and began to splash through the water. He pulled himself out of the water as he reached the shore and streaked toward the sumac that rose a dozen feet away.

Two very wild shots whistled through the air, but he had reached the trees and plunged into the dark denseness of the smooth-surfaced leaves. He moved into the trees for a few feet and then dropped low as the two horsemen reined up. "Go in after the bastard," he heard Joe order. "I'll go right, you go left." Fargo, crouched on one knee behind the thick screen of leaves, caught sight

46

of the two horsemen as they nosed their mounts into the trees. He waited, holding his breath, as one rider moved closer to him, then cast a quick glance at the other pursuer moving slowly some dozen feet back. The nearest horseman came opposite him, the man holding his gun as he strained to see through the sumac, inching the horse forward. Fargo let him go almost all the way past before he sprang into motion.

Uncoiling his body with the silent speed of a powerful mountain lion, he sprang from his crouch, hurling himself upward. His hand closed around the man's wrist and he pulled. The man flew sideways from the saddle as Fargo's other hand wrapped around his neck. As he landed on the ground, Fargo stomped onto his gun hand, and the man let out a scream of pain. It ended instantly as Fargo's knee came down on his throat. Fargo threw himself flat as a shot whistled over his head from behind him. As he flattened himself on the ground, he yanked the pistol from the man's lifeless fingers, rolled, and fired two shots at the rider coming toward him through the trees. Both missed as he fired in haste. But the shots did what he wanted; the rider turned the horse to race away, suddenly aware he was now the target. Fargo, handling a gun with which he was unfamiliar, steadied his arm against a low branch.

He took aim, followed the fleeing rider, and fired two quick shots. "Jesus," the man cried out in pain, and Fargo saw him fall from the saddle. Running forward, Fargo reached the figure on the ground and saw the man clutching his shoulder with his gun still in his hand.

"Drop the gun, Joe," Fargo said, and the man let the gun fall from his hand. "Now stand up," Fargo ordered.

"My shoulder . . . Jesus, it hurts," the man said, but

pushed to his feet. Fargo saw his Colt in the man's waist, reached out, and pulled the gun from him.

"This is mine," Fargo said. "Start walking."

"My shoulder's killing me," the man said.

"You don't walk on your shoulder," Fargo said as he tossed the other pistol aside and held the Colt. The man started to walk, still holding his upper arm, moved away from the trees, and onto the open land of the lake shore where he halted. He turned as a red stain spread from his shoulder and saw Fargo facing him with the Colt raised to fire. "Now, Joe, remember how you were going to drown me in the lake? Well, that's sure as hell what I'm going to do to you unless you start talking," Fargo said almost pleasantly.

"I told you, I don't know anything," Joe said, a whine in his voice.

"You said a man named Kosta hired you. Start there. Tell me about him. What's he look like?" Fargo questioned.

"I don't know," Joe said.

Fargo looked disappointed. "You in a hurry to touch bottom, Joe? You talked to him, but you don't know what he looked like?"

"He wore a mask, a cloth that covered his face. It made him talk funny. I had trouble understanding him," Joe said.

"But his name was Kosta.

"That's what he said."

"Tall, short, fat, thin?" Fargo queried.

"Medium build," the man said.

"What else did he say?"

"He paid me the money, told me to pick my own men," Joe said.

"Someone put him onto you. Who would that be?" Fargo asked.

"Could've been three or four people," the man said.

"I'll buy that," Fargo grunted. "How'd you know where to meet him? Somebody had to tell you."

"There was a note left for me, at the saloon," Joe said.

"Then we'll pay a visit to the saloon. Maybe the barkeep has a better memory than you," Fargo said. "Wait there," he added and walked to the water's edge where the lifeless figure lay almost in the water. He bent down and retrieved the thin-bladed throwing knife, wiped it clean, and had just returned it to its calf-holster when a shot rang out. Fargo dropped onto his stomach as the bullet grazed his hair, rolled, and barely avoided another bullet. But he had the Colt raised, and he fired a single shot, and Joe clutched his abdomen this time as he pitched forward facedown onto the soft sand. He had taken the gun from one of the other figures sprawled nearby, and Fargo swore at his own carelessness. He walked to the man and holstered the Colt. There was no reason to visit the saloon now.

He walked to the pinto, pulled himself onto the horse, and rode away, thoughts pushing against each other. Whoever had hired the would-be killers had been careful and clever, and as he rode, he began to sort out what remained unanswered and the question that had been answered. When he finally neared Dennison, he turned short of the town and went up the low hill to the cluster of hawthorns where he undressed, wrung out his wet clothes, and hung them on low branches to dry. The moon was high when he stretched out on the bedroll after drying himself with a towel from his saddlebag. If Brenda or any of the others had come looking for him, they'd wonder where he was, of course. They'd learn in time, he grunted silently and let sleep come to him.

He gave the morning sun an extra hour to finish drying his clothes before he washed and dressed and rode to Dennison. The half circle of wagons was a hub of activity, and Derek Hogath handed him a mug of freshly brewed coffee. "They'll all be ready in another hour or two," the man said, his voice resounding with confident anticipation.

"Good," Fargo said and decided to wait a little longer before confronting Hogath with what he had painfully learned. He strolled on, sipping his coffee, and came to a halt where Alison wrestled with a knot in a rope at the tailgate of her wagon. She paused to turn cool eyes on him.

"Enjoy last night? Cindy her usual willing self?" she remarked with an edge of tartness.

He let his lips purse as he turned the remark in his mind and took a moment to enjoy the curve of her breasts under a tan shirt. "You always assume things?" he asked.

"Let's call it an educated guess," she said.

"Let's call it bullshit, honey." He smiled. "You came calling."

"Now who's assuming?" she countered, and he allowed her a smile. She was quick-minded as well as sharp-tongued. He let his glance move inside the wagon and felt a tiny furrow touch his brow. Instead of the interior jammed with boxes, barrels, furniture, trunks, and all the household materials that filled most wagons, he saw only a cot at one side, one trunk, and a few clothing boxes.

"You're traveling real light for someone who figures

to settle down and stay," he commented and saw the flash of annoyance that touched her face before she could wipe it away.

"How observant," she said and sniffed.

"Occupational disease," he said, watching her.

"We're all traveling light. We're going to share things when we settle in," she said. "Something wrong with that?"

"Your call," he said.

"Your cynical streak is showing again," she said.

"Sorry about that," he said and walked on, feeling her eyes boring into him. He passed the army compound and paused where Lieutenant Bowdon prepared to take out a patrol. "How's the major? Still steamed?" Fargo asked.

"You can bet on it. The major doesn't take kindly to having his requests turned down," Bowdon said.

"Tell him I'll be out of his hair. I'll be breaking new trails," Fargo said.

"I have the impression he doesn't care much what happens to you. He's busy preparing to be the commander of Fort Sanders," the lieutenant said.

"You share his views, Lieutenant?" Fargo asked.

Bowdon kept his face set. "I'd give you an escort part of the way. I think that's the right thing to do. But lieutenants don't disagree with majors," he said.

"That's right, but thanks for the thought," Fargo said and walked on, the Ovaro following at his heels. He saw the thin, reedy figure in the army boots, Indian shawl, and tattered britches standing at a corner of the compound. The man watched him go by, his broad-cheeked face impassive. Fargo continued on to the back side of the stockade wall, took a dandy brush and stable sponge from his saddlebag, and, using water from his canteen, gave the Ovaro a thorough grooming, ending with the hoof pick. When he finished, he made his way back to the wagons. Lieutenant Bowdon had taken out his patrol, but the thin, black-haired figure of the Indian scout was still standing at the edge of the compound.

The sun had started past the noon hour, Fargo noted, when he reached the wagons. "Ready to go, Fargo," Derek Hogath called, and Fargo rode past Alison atop her wagon. Brenda Jackson tossed him a broad smile from the second wagon, and Pearl Smith held the reins of the third wagon with Ida Bluebell beside her. He rode to the front of the group where Derek Hogath waited. "Let's roll," he said, and with a small cheer the others moved after him. He rode north, turned northeast when he passed the low hills, and continued on, turning north again. The sun was dropping over the distant mountains when he reached the North Platte, and they made camp at the river's edge. The wagons stretched out in a line along the shore, and evening meals were prepared with the added gift of water that needed no rationing.

Fargo accepted Hogath's invitation to eat with him and a family named Epson. It was only when the meal was finished and the wagons settling down for the night that he called Hogath and Alison to his side. "You two are running your respective trains, and I didn't see any good to come of making everyone nervous, but I've something to tell you," he began. "Some very unpleasant gents tried to kill me." He saw Hogath and Alison both react in shock. "They wanted to make sure I didn't get you through."

"Why, in God's name? What's it mean?" Derek Hogath breathed.

"Don't know," Fargo said. "You ever hear of a man named Kosta?" he asked Hogath.

"Kosta? No, why?" Hogath questioned.

"He hired the sidewinders who tried to kill me. One of them said the man's name was Kosta, and he wore a cloth over his head," Fargo answered.

"Never heard of him. But I'm not the only man who takes settlers to choice locations for a fee. Whoever gets to settle in first gets the best land and becomes the foundation stones of a new community. The more groups you get to a location first, the more other groups will hire you. Maybe this Kosta has a group he wants to bring to Fort Sanders first. If I don't make it, he's got clear sailing for himself and his group."

The answer had reasonableness, yet it failed to satisfy him, and Fargo frowned into space. "In that attack I'd swear they were looking for something. Everything in that wagon train had been emptied and searched through," he said.

"Then the attempt to kill you means they didn't find whatever they were looking for," Hogath said.

"It also means all those poor people were killed for something they weren't carrying," Fargo said.

"My God," Hogath said, anguish in his voice.

"But we don't know. We're speculating," Fargo said.

"That's right. Were they looking for something in those wagons, or were they just out to stop us from getting to Fort Sanders?" Hogath asked.

"Or both," Fargo said, and Hogath stared back.

"Both? How could it be both?" Hogath asked.

"I don't have any idea, but if we're speculating, we might as well speculate all the way," Fargo replied.

"Whatever the reason, does this mean we can expect another attack?" Hogath wondered aloud.

"They've gone this far. I don't see them just backing off," Fargo said.

"You were absolutely right about the first attack. They were fake Cheyenne. At least we won't have to be concerned with Indians," Hogath said.

"I wouldn't say that. We'll be in Cheyenne territory soon enough. You can damn well be concerned about the real ones," Fargo said and cast a glance at Alison. "You haven't said a word," he commented.

There was pain in her blue eyes as she met his stare. "Didn't see there was much to say," she answered.

"Guess not," he agreed. "Now let's get some sleep." He rose and walked back to the Ovaro, led the horse away from the wagons and under the wide-spread branches of a peachleaf willow a few thousand yards away. He had just undressed and lay on his bedroll when a figure appeared, blanket in hand, clad in a nightdress that reached only to her knees. Alison set the blanket down a few feet from him.

"Something wrong with that cot in your wagon?" he asked.

"I find it stuffy sleeping inside the wagon," she said, settling herself on the blanket. "But I wouldn't go off by myself to sleep. You make the perfect compromise."

He watched her with a half smile edging his lips. "That's a good answer, all nice and reasonable. Only I'm not sure it's the right one," he said.

She leaned on one elbow, and he saw the lovely curve of one full breast trying to escape the top scoop of the nightdress. "What are you implying?" Alison frowned.

"It's certainly not because I couldn't resist being near you."

"Didn't say it was," Fargo said blandly.

"Then what are you saying?" she snapped.

He put his arms behind his head as she watched him stretch the muscled smoothness of his body. "I had a big-footed, flop-eared dog once, half Saint Bernard and half Blue-tick hound. Anytime I'd lay down, he'd come and lay down right close. It wasn't that he couldn't resist being near me. He just didn't want anybody else near me. Best damn watchdog I ever had."

"You just can't help being suspicious about everything, can you?" Alison shot back.

"It's hard. I hate myself," he tossed at her.

"As I'm neither big-footed nor flop-eared, I don't fit the description of a watchdog," she said.

"I guess being right two out of three isn't bad," he returned.

"You're impossible," Alison said, then turned with a flounce, and he enjoyed the way her breasts jiggled. It took her a while before she stopped seething and fidgeting and fell asleep. He watched the moon trail across the deep blue velvet sky and made plans for the next day's travel until he finally dropped off to sleep.

When he woke with the new day, Alison was still asleep, the top of the nightdress pulled to one side, and the loveliness of one breast lay almost entirely exposed, round and made of creamy curves. Asleep, all the starchy stiffness gone from her, she had a sweetness to her face that surprised him. He walked to the river, wondering why she felt the need to mask that with self-contained control. But she did. That much was increasingly obvious. Bedding down beside him was only one example. She was plainly not inclined to let Brenda pay him another late-night visit, or any of the other two young women. It was fun to think she was being jealous, but he knew that played little part in it. But something told him it was more than just protectiveness. That, too, was a part of the mask she put on. Something about Alison and her little troupe of midwives still refused to sit right, but his thoughts broke off as he heard her rise. He finished washing, looked around, and saw her starting off toward the distant wagons, the blanket half wrapped around her.

"Come again," he called, and she tossed him a quick glare, all the stiffness back in her face. Yet in the undignified wrappings there was still a handsome attractiveness to her, back held straight, thighs vibrantly full under the thin garment, dark blond hair trailing behind her sharply cheekboned face. Fargo finished dressing and strolled back to the wagons where he shared a mug of coffee with Derek Hogath.

"Couldn't say I slept well last night," Hogath said. "I feel somewhat traitorous not telling the others."

"They won't be any better for going on in fear," Fargo said.

"Guess not," Hogath conceded unhappily, and Fargo finished his coffee to find Brenda and Pearl waiting as he crossed near their wagon. Both glanced at him with expressions that were a combination of apology and sullenness.

"She can be such a bitch," Brenda hissed. "She treats us like schoolgirls."

"You let her," Fargo said, and both young women tightened their faces at once.

"We owe her," Pearl said, and both grew very quiet.

"You're grateful to her for what she's taught you?" Fargo probed.

"Something like that," Pearl said, not looking at him.

"Dedicated people can be so intense," Brenda said, exasperation in her voice, and Fargo found himself again wondering about Alison and the three young women. It was plainly an involved relationship. They seemed to see her as many things—teacher, leader, surrogate mother, guardian, and as another female with all the elements of rivalry that were part of such relationships. But there was something more, he told himself. The story of the midwives still refused to hang right inside him, but again he put it aside. Alison stepped firmly from her wagon to see to her horses, and Fargo strolled away. He moved the wagons forward as soon as the people had all breakfasted, carefully crossed the Platte, and led the way west through thickly forested hill country.

He had decided to stay longer in Wyoming territory before crossing into the Dakotas, and he rode ahead, discovering half-hidden passages the wagons could negotiate. He stayed away from large open spaces and riding ahead, he paused at a high ledge and watched the caravan move past below. Many of the youngsters ran and played outside the wagons, he noted, but they all seemed a well-disciplined group, and he was comforted by that. Discipline could spell the difference between death and survival in this country. Alison's three wagons brought up the rear of the train, and he saw that she had changed to riding her extra horse, the tall-legged gelding she'd had the first time he met her. Ida Bluebell drove the last wagon. When Alison spied him on the ledge, she sent the gelding up to where he waited.

"Mind company?" she asked.

"No," he said, and she swung alongside him as he left the ledge, rode on, and found a long, narrow defile where he pulled up and waved the wagons into the passage. He rode on again, knowing they'd be in the passage for hours, and as he climbed out of the defile, he moved up a low hill. Alison stayed alongside him as he paused atop the hill and surveyed a series of three long rises.

"You're keeping the wagons in narrow passages and defiles. Why?" she asked.

"They'd be more easily noticed in open land and even more easily attacked," Fargo answered and sent the horse forward over the next rise. Alison beside him, he had crossed the third rise when he saw a plume of dust rise up beyond the next ridge, and Alison pulled the gelding closer.

"Indians," she breathed, alarm in her voice, and Fargo let his eyes narrow as he watched the plume travel in front of them.

"No," he said finally and sent the Ovaro forward. Alison caught up to him at once and stayed close beside him as he crested the rise and reined to a halt. The line of blue-clad troopers passed just below, Lieutenant Bowdon riding at the head of the column of twos.

"How'd you know?" Alison asked, awe in her voice.

"Signatures. They come in all forms," Fargo said. She frowned back. "Every smoke column is different, its own signature. This column is steady, neat, no variation in it, moving in a straight line at a disciplined pace, completely contained, no stray whirls. Only the cavalry sends up such a neat column of smoke." The awe stayed in Alison's face as she followed him down the slope where the lieutenant pulled his troop to a halt. "Afternoon, Lieutenant," Fargo said. "You're far beyond your usual rounds, aren't you?"

"Yes, sir. The major's orders. He's had us on overnight field patrol," Bowdon said.

"Don't tell me he's grown concerned over us," Fargo said.

Lieutenant Bowdon grimaced. "I'm afraid not, sir," he answered. "My orders are to make sweeping patrols, show the colors, let the hostiles see us. He figures if they see us as a real presence, they'll lay low, and that'll make it easier for him to escort the officials without real trouble."

Fargo pursed his lips. "That might work. But he's sending you out on a limb."

"That's what the army pays us to do," the lieutenant said with the wry dedication of a career officer.

"Good luck, Lieutenant," Fargo said. "Maybe we'll cross paths again."

"It's possible," Bowdon said and sent his patrol forward at a slow trot. Fargo watched the column disappear over the hills and then turned with Alison and headed back to meet the wagons as they emerged from the defile. Alison left his side to return to where Brenda drove the lead wagon, and Fargo led the way to a spot between two clusters of black oak as the day drew to a close. The area large enough for everyone to find a spot, he dismounted as the others unhitched horses and prepared to eat. He shared a meal with Derek Hogath and then took his bedroll into the northernmost cluster of trees, undressed, and stretched out in the warm night. He had almost wagered with himself when Alison appeared with her blanket, this time wearing a full-length nightdress of silk that clung to her body, outlining the fullness of every part of it. She halted, and he saw her eyes move over his near-naked, muscled contours, finally halting at his face.

"You expected me?" she asked.

"Did I say that?" he answered.

"That little smile on your face," she said and put the blanket on the ground.

"Closer," he said.

"Why?" she asked, though she brought the blanket within arm's length of him.

"I might as well enjoy looking, too," he said, and she tossed him a glare. "You going to use the same excuse for tonight?" he asked casually.

"It's not an excuse," she snapped.

He smiled at her. "Call it whatever you like. You're here to see that Brenda, Ida, and Pearl aren't."

"I am not. That's your suspicious nature talking," Alison said, and he was surprised at how indignant she managed to sound.

"Seems to me you're the one who's suspicious," Fargo tossed at her.

"I'm not suspicious. I'm concerned. I don't want them getting into the kind of relationships you're all too willing to enjoy," Alison said.

"Maybe they'd like to," he said.

"Then they can do it afterward," Alison snapped.

"Afterward?" he echoed and saw her lips tighten.

"When they're on their own. When they're no longer my responsibility," she said quickly. He turned the reply in his mind. Perhaps she had more of the mother hen in her than he'd guessed. Or perhaps there was something more. Alison's answers to everything were cloaked in a reasonableness that never completely satisfied. He decided to push her a little more.

"That still makes me right. You're here so they don't come visiting," Fargo said.

"I just told you why," Alison said, resting on one elbow, her breasts dipping to one side in a graceful curve.

"I heard. Responsibility. Concern. Big words can be excuses. Maybe you've fooled yourself into believing them," he said.

"That's ridiculous." She frowned.

"Is it?" he said and leaned over, his arm brushing the tops of her breasts as he brought his mouth down on hers. She gave a little startled gasp, but didn't move as he pressed the softness of her lips. When he drew back, his arm again rubbed the two tiny points. He saw her lips stay open for a long moment before she pulled them closed.

"Satisfied?" she muttered, swallowing hard.

"Very much," he said.

She frowned back. "What's that mean?"

"I'll stick with excuses," he said, lying back on the bedroll.

"Nonsense," she hissed, turned on her side, her back to him, and pulled the blanket around herself. He smiled as he closed his eyes. Alison Carter clung to her own agenda, whatever it was.

4

She woke with him as the morning sun dawned, and he watched her gather the blanket to herself, dark blond hair falling loosely around her face to give her a softness she ordinarily masked. She paused and peered at him. "Sometimes people have good reasons for what they do," she said and managed to sound genuinely hurt.

"Most often they act more than think," he said.

"Stop being so damn cynical," she snapped.

"Give me a reason," he said, and she spun on her heel and strode away, dark blond hair trailing behind her, long, full-thighed legs beautifully outlined as the silk nightdress clung. Fargo rose, used his canteen water to wash, and joined the others when he finished dressing. He saddled the Ovaro, looked over the wagons, and saw they were all hitched and ready to move. Alison, dressed in black skirt and white shirt, held the reins of her wagon and tossed him a coolly contained glance he thought edged with smugness.

He led the wagons forward with a wave and continued to stay away from open land whenever he could. Riding ahead, he scanned the terrain and swore at the number of Indian pony prints he spotted. Finding a narrow valley with a heavy border of bur oak, he scouted both sides before he waved the wagons into it. They'd be hours moving through the valley, so he rode on again, this time climbing the forested sides until he was in low hills well covered with black oak and cottonwoods. The afternoon sky rose over him as he turned and met the train as it emerged from the valley. They were into Wyoming territory, he knew as he saw Horse Creek and took the wagons across the curving waterway in single file. He swung eastward when they had crossed to eventually move into the Dakotas. The rolling hills held enough passages between them for the wagons to negotiate, and once again Fargo rode ahead and climbed into the hills. He had come onto a ridge when he caught movement on the hillside in front of him, leaves suddenly moving, a soft rustling sound.

His hand on the Colt at his hip, he rode forward, saw the leaves move again, and then glimpsed the figure of the horseman through the heavy oak branches. The rider began to move down the other side of the hill, increasing his speed, and Fargo gave chase. He let the Ovaro have his head, the horse skirting through narrow spaces between the trees, using its powerful, jet black hindquarters to barely slow its pace. He was closing on the fleeing horseman and saw the rider swerve and plunge down a deer trail to his right. Fargo followed, saw the man glance back at him again, then disappear into a thick cluster of branches and reappear a few yards below.

The Ovaro continued to close in on the fleeing rider, and suddenly the horseman reined his mount in and leaped from its back. Fargo pulled the pinto to a halt and slid from the saddle before he became an open target. He crouched on the ground, listened to the man's horse come to a halt and the silence settle over the woods. Colt in hand, Fargo waited and finally caught the soft sound of a footstep brushing leaves. Fargo listened again, then followed the sound as it came again. Though he kept the revolver in hand, he didn't want to use it, not with all the Indian pony prints he'd seen. Besides, he wanted the man alive. The rider had seen him and instantly fled. Until then he'd been scouting the terrain. Looking for what? Fargo paused, listened again, and heard the figure moving toward his horse. Fargo quickened his steps, but stayed noiselessly on the balls of his feet. The trees suddenly thinned, and Fargo saw the man almost at his horse. Discarding silence, Fargo bolted forward, the Colt raised, and reached the end of the trees as the man came to his horse.

The man didn't know he was unwilling to use the Colt, and Fargo raised the gun as he called out. "You're a dead man," he said and saw the man freeze, one hand on his saddle horn. "Don't do anything stupid," Fargo said as he stepped from the trees into the open area of the slope. The man stayed motionless, and Fargo started to step closer when a sharp scream cut through the air. He recognized Alison's voice immediately, and his eyes snapped to where the scream had come from halfway down the slope. He saw her, on the ground where she'd been thrown from the gelding who'd raced away. Only a few feet from her the long, coiled form of a big timber rattler jay poised to strike. Out of the corners of his eyes Fargo saw the man instantly take in the scene and pull himself onto his horse.

Fargo cursed silently as the man sent his horse racing away. A shot would certainly trigger the rattler's strike, and he continued to curse as the man rode away down the slope and into the trees at his right. The hoofbeats died away, and the only sound left was the loud, angry hiss of the snake's rattle filling the air. Fargo swore again. If he ran to the Ovaro and pursued the horseman, Alison was dead. The rattler was coiled, rattling furiously, one big, angry snake, seconds away from striking. With a surge of anger and bitterness welling up inside him, Fargo knew he had really no choice left to him. But he still wanted no shots, and as he slid his foot forward, he holstered the Colt and drew the thin-bladed throwing knife from its calf-holster.

Alison's eyes were round with terror as she sat before the snake, whose forked tongue flicked out again. Luckily for her, terror had frozen her in place. A blink of an eye and the rattler would already have struck. But even frozen time was running out for Alison. The snake's rattle had grown still louder, its flicking tongue the sensory weapon for its deadly strike. Fargo raised his arm and took aim, grateful that the rattler was the large, thick-bodied specimen it was. With a quick, overhand motion, using all the power in his wrist and forearm, he flung the blade. He offered a silent prayer as the thin shaft hurtled through the air. His lips pulled back, and he felt the cry of triumph spiral from his throat as the blade struck the rattler just behind its head. It came out the other side of the snake, stopped from going all the way through only by the blade's hilt.

The snake's coils leaped upward and flung themselves in whipping circles in midair, back and forth in a sinuous paroxysm of death. Fargo heard Alison's cry as, the spell broken, she fell backward, and the leaping, twisting coils continued to flail the air until, with a shuddering motion, the long diamond-marked body finally fell to the ground, twitched a moment more, and lay still. Fargo moved toward her as she leaped up and in seconds she was against him, all the full softness of her clinging to him, trembling violently. He held her and felt the roundness of her breasts pressing into him, the slight convexity of her belly tight against him. Her face pressed against his neck, lips open against him, her skin smooth, and he smelled the faint scent of powder. Her breath came in soft gasps, and when she drew back, her lips stayed parted, her eyes round as the terror slowly receded from her. "Thank you," she murmured. "God, thank you," and suddenly her mouth was on his, open, wet, pressing hard, and he let her lips push against his until finally she pulled away again. "I'm sorry," she said, pulling her mouth closed and her face into a semblance of propriety.

"I'm not," he said.

"It was a reaction, a perfectly natural reaction," she murmured.

"Absolutely," he said blandly. "Now what the hell were you doing up here?" Fargo asked, his voice hardening.

"I decided to go riding by myself. I guess I thought I might find you," she said.

"You did, dammit, and because of you that son of a bitch got away," Fargo said.

"I'm sorry. How could I know a rattler would spook my horse?" she said.

"Nobody leaves the wagons from now on without my permission," Fargo muttered.

"Who was he?" Alison asked as she walked to where the gelding waited at the edge of the bottom of the slope.

"I was about to find out until you showed up," Fargo said bitterly.

"You think he was looking for us?" Alison asked.

"Let's hope it was something else, but he was scouting up here and didn't want to be asked what for," Fargo said, then bent over and retrieved the throwing blade, wiped it clean, and swung onto the Ovaro. Alison rode at his side, and then went down the slope and joined the wagons as the day began to draw to an end. He led the way to a spot at the edge of a line of red cedar that afforded good cover. When the evening meal ended and the moon had come up, he gathered his bedroll to find Alison at his side.

"I want to thank you again. I'd be dead of snakebite if it wasn't for you," she said, her eyes round with grateful sincerity.

"That's true," he said and saw exasperation come into her face.

"You don't have to rub it in," she said, and her eyes went to the bedroll under his arm. "I won't be coming to bed down," she said.

His brows lifted as he gazed at her. "Change of heart? Suddenly no more watchdog?"

She shrugged. "Call it whatever you like," she said.

"What happened to seeing that the girls stay out of trouble?" Fargo asked.

"I decided to trust they'll do that," Alison said, turned, and started to walk away when he caught her arm.

"Know what I'm thinking? It's yourself you don't trust, especially after this afternoon," he said.

"That's not it at all." She sniffed, but he saw the two spots of color redden her cheeks, visible even in the moonlight. He let go of her arm, and she strode away, back stiff, soft rear swaying.

"Didn't your mother tell you it's not nice to lie?" he

called after her, but she refused to reply, and he smiled as she disappeared into her wagon. He went on with his bedroll, undressed, and stretched out. He went to sleep, still wondering about the horseman in the hills.

When morning came, he led the wagons northwest and estimated another day would bring them to the edge of the Black Hills. Fort Sanders would be only another two days away, and he allowed himself a sliver of optimism as the day proceeded with no problems. Only the Indian pony tracks continued to alarm him, and he carefully searched the terrain ahead of the wagons, still keeping to hill passages with good tree cover. He circled back to the wagons to lead them through a lush valley heavily grown with the thick, spreading branches of bur oak. He rode ahead again once they were in the valley and drew to a halt where the land rose upward to become a mountain path bordered on one side by a sheer drop.

He grimaced, but saw that the path was plenty wide enough for the wagons and shielded on one side by a high wall of brush-covered rock. He turned and rode back to the wagons as the day began to slide toward dusk and had just reached Derek Hogath in the lead wagon when he peered down the length of the valley at the sound and saw the column of blue-clad troopers coming up from the rear. He waved the wagons to a halt, and the troopers rode to a halt alongside the wagons. No earnest, young Lieutenant Bowdon, he saw, but a heavy-jowled face wearing a two-day stubble and a uniform that had trouble fitting around the midsection. Fargo's glance flicked along the rest of the column. Some had more trouble fitting their uniforms than the lieutenant, and a few needed a fit at least a size smaller. One of the troopers carried the Troop C pennant, Fargo noted. "Lieutenant Clancy," the officer said.

"What happened to Lieutenant Bowdon?" Fargo asked.

"He was ordered back to Dennison to help escort the official party," Lieutenant Clancy said. "We've taken over here. In fact, we've orders to see you safely to Fort Sanders."

Fargo felt his brows lift. "Well, that's a change. What made the major change his mind?" he queried.

"You'll have to ask him when you see him," the lieutenant replied. "We'll just ride along with you for now." Fargo nodded, and again his eyes swept the column of troopers. "Half you men ride up front, the others ride behind," Clancy ordered his men, and Fargo saw the troopers carrying the company pennant hand it to one of the other men as he moved forward.

"We'll be making camp before we get out of the valley. There's a good spot a mile or so on," Fargo told the lieutenant.

"Whatever you say," the officer answered and rose on to join the forward half of his men. Fargo watched him ride away as he brought the Ovaro alongside Hogath.

"We'll make camp in a tight circle," he said to Hogath.

The man frowned. "You expect an Indian attack with the patrol here?" he asked. "It sure makes me feel better to have them along."

"A tight circle," Fargo answered and dropped back and let the wagons pass him. He drew waves and smiles from Brenda and Pearl and caught Alison's questioning frown. Listening and watching him had heightened her already sharp instincts, he grunted silently and ignored the glance. The troopers at the rear of the wagons passed him, and he nodded at the men as they went by. Another of the troopers carried the company pennant, he noted. He put the Ovaro into a trot, passed the wagons, and caught up to Lieutenant Clancy at the front of his patrol. Swinging in beside the officer, he kept his tone casual. "You know this territory, Lieutenant?" he asked.

"Some," the lieutenant answered.

"The army have a name for the region around the Black Hills?" Fargo questioned.

"That's all Dakota territory," Clancy said.

"That what we're in now?" Fargo pressed.

"That's right," the officer said. Fargo tossed him a smile as he moved the Ovaro forward.

"Much obliged," he said and rode ahead until dusk began to slide across an expanse of Jerusalem artichokes, turning their large, golden yellow leaves into a pale amber. He found the spot he sought and waited for the others to come up, where he directed the wagons to a flat area backed by a stand of bur oak. Lieutenant Clancy drew his troops to one side, and Fargo watched Derek Hogath obey his orders and draw the wagons into a tight circle. Night had begun to replace dusk when everyone had settled in and the evening meal had begun. Fargo's gaze went to where the troopers were bedding down in a rough line a few dozen yards from the wagons. As he unsaddled the Ovaro, he watched the soldiers tether their mounts to nearby low branches, then lay down with their carbines at their sides. Finally, he turned away and strolled to Derek Hogath and found Alison there. She watched him approach with the same questioning frown she wore when she had passed him earlier.

"You're bothered," she said to him as he halted. "I was just telling that to Mister Hogath."

"You're getting too sharp, Alison," Fargo grunted. "Yes, I'm bothered, real bothered." He turned to Derek Hogath, his jaw set tight. "No sense in keeping folks from getting a good night's sleep, but tomorrow morning you'll give your people an order, a rotten, cold-blooded order that'll spell the difference between life and death for them."

Hogath stared at him, his jaw dropping open. "Good God, Fargo. What's all this about?"

"It's about those soldier boys. They're ringers," Fargo said. "They're wearing cavalry uniforms, but they're not army."

"What in tarnation makes you say a thing like that? I hope it's not because their uniforms fit badly. The army always has a problem with uniforms. Hell, I've seen lots of soldiers in uniforms that don't fit right," Derek Hogath said.

"Me, too. I could go with that, but nothing about this crew fits," Fargo said.

"Such as?" Hogath probed.

"For starters, they don't sit their horses the way a cavalry trooper sits a horse. They don't have any snap in the saddle. Then, a company pennant is always carried up front, never in the rear, and it's always carried by one particular trooper assigned to carry it, kind of an honor. These pass it around from one to the other. No cavalry troop would do that. I watched them bed down. They settled down any old place. A cavalry troop beds down in a line or a half circle, almost by twos, the way they ride. They're keeping their carbines with them as they sleep. Unless it's in imminent danger of attack, a troop stacks their carbines in a pyramid in front of their tents

71

or wherever they bed down. That's just army procedure."

"There's more?" Hogath breathed as Fargo paused, his eyes round.

"Yes." Fargo nodded. "The army has its own way of saying things. It becomes part of how they give and take orders. That's especially true of officers. I heard this Lieutenant Clancy tell his men, 'Half of you ride up front, the others ride behind.'" Fargo uttered a snort of derision. "No cavalry officer would give a command like that. He'd say, 'Ten troopers forward, ten to the rear.'"

Hogath let a long breath escape him. "Yes, I've heard that often enough," he said.

"I asked this Lieutenant Clancy if the army has a name for the region around the Black Hills. Just Dakota territory, he said. I asked him if that's where we were now and he said yes, it was all Dakota territory. Well, the army designates everything from just below the Black Hills to the Canadian border as the Department of Dakota. They call where we are now the Department of the Platte. I don't know who Clancy and his men are, but I know who they're not."

"How'd they get the uniforms?" Alison asked.

Fargo's face grew grim. "You don't want to even think about that, not now," he said.

"If they're here to kill us, what are they waiting for?" she queried.

"The right spot. Someplace nobody's going to stumble onto us soon. I'm afraid that place is waiting for them up ahead," Fargo answered.

"What do you want me to do?" Hogath asked.

"In the morning you go from wagon to wagon. They'll see you, but it'll seem ordinary enough. Very quietly, you tell each of the wagons to pick out one of those phony troopers and be ready to shoot him when the time comes. Tell them to be prepared to do it no matter how cold-blooded it seems. If they don't, they're all dead. Tell them you'll explain later," Fargo said. "I'll pick the moment. When I shoot, they shoot. Got it?"

"Understood," Hogath said, and Fargo got to his feet.

"Get some sleep now," he said, and Alison, her face pulled tight, didn't glance at him as she strode away. Fargo walked only a few yards away before setting down his bedroll, and he forced himself to sleep. When the new day came, he woke, washed, and dressed, then watched the fake troopers come awake. He saddled the Ovaro, an eerie feeling churning inside him, a man aware of what was going to happen and unable to change the course of events as they moved to an inexorable conclusion. He saw Hogath, a mug of coffee in hand, moving from wagon to wagon, and was able to draw a glimmer of comfort from that. The lieutenant had most of his men up and ready to ride, Fargo noted and swung onto the Ovaro. He walked the horse to where Clancy prepared to mount up and saw the man quickly button the top of his uniform. Fargo smiled inwardly at the attempt to play a role. "We'll be moving out of the valley and up along a deep gorge," Fargo said and saw the man's eyes light. "You'll be riding on ahead to scout?" Fargo asked casually.

"Later," Clancy said. "For now we'll just ride along behind. Any Indians see you, they'll see us."

"That's real comforting," Fargo said and smiled, then returned to where Derek Hogath sat with reins in hand. "Finished your inspection?" he asked.

"Yes," Hogath said, his face grave. Fargo waved the

73

train forward and sent the Ovaro out ahead, watching as the column of troopers fell in at the rear. More than wagon wheels were turning, he grunted. The wheels of fate turned, the promise of death turned, and with it the swirl of desperate hope. Fargo rode forward, changed into a trot, and it was all too soon that he was upon the pathway that rose slowly upward with the sheer gorge dropping off at one side, the high wall of rock at the other. He stopped, dismounted, and peered down into the gorge. The bottom was overgrown with heavy tree growth, mostly hackberry, he saw, with jutting pinnacles of volcanic rock among the trees.

Broken wagons down there would simply disappear, he muttered and swung back onto the horse to wait. The noon sun was high in the sky when the wagons reached the spot, and he waved them forward. The curving path was more than wide enough for the wagons and a line of horsemen to move along together, and he saw Lieutenant Clancy lean from his saddle to peer into the gorge. Fargo let a grim sound escape him as the officer immediately turned to his men, barked at them, and began to move up alongside the line of wagons at a fast trot. Fargo moved the Ovaro between Alison's wagon and the Conestoga in front of her and caught the fear in the glance she gave him. His quick nod was a silent answer, and he saw her drop the reins and climb into the wagon. He glimpsed her at the front, just inside the edge of the opening, an old Hawkens plains rifle in her hands. His eyes went to the front of the line of wagons, saw Clancy reach a spot just ahead of Hogath's Conestoga, and Fargo drew the big Henry from its saddlebag. There was no question in his mind about what he had to do, just as he had no question of what Clancy was about to do. He brought the

Henry to his shoulder, edged the Ovaro forward, and fired.

The fake lieutenant had started to turn, and the shot caught him in the left shoulder. The heavy rifle slug had both power and weight, and he barely avoided falling from his horse. His men reined up, taken by surprise, and before they had a chance to gather themselves, the wagons erupted in a fusillade of gunfire. Fargo saw at least ten of the blue-clad figures fall from their horses, most hitting the edge of the passage, bouncing off to plummet down the steep side of the gorge. Others tried to fire back, but the gunfire continued from the wagons, and the fake soldiers could muster only a few shots before more were cut down. Fargo's glance went to the lieutenant and saw the man had sent his horse racing up the rest of the passage. Fargo brought the Ovaro out to the edge of the drop and gave chase as Clancy disappeared around the long curve. But he was still fleeing, the sound of his hoofbeats clear on the rock of the passage.

Fargo rounded the curve and saw the man moving to the end of the passage where the land opened onto a high plain. He let the pinto close distance and brought his rifle to his shoulder again before he called out. "Stop, and you can stay alive," he shouted. The man's answer was to turn in the saddle with a big Remington revolver in his right hand. He fired two shots, both uncomfortably close. Fargo's finger squeezed the trigger, and the Henry erupted again. This time the man bucked in the saddle before he fell to lay still, half on what remained of his chest. Fargo halted, stared down at the figure, and knew it would be a waste of time to search the man. He turned the pinto and started back down the passage, aware that the sounds of shots had ended. The line of wagons were stopped as he reached them, half of their occupants on the ground. "Anybody hurt?" he asked.

"Three flesh wounds," Hogath said. "They're being tended to now."

"You did real well," Fargo said. "I know it was hard for you to shoot down people in cold blood. But it was the only way, or they'd have killed all of you. We had to strike first." They nodded, faces grave. They had survived, but they were shaken by it, all of them, men, women, and children, all draped in silence. "We'll be moving on. We'll talk when we pull up for the night. Take their horses. The army will appreciate getting them back."

He turned to go when Alison's voice cut in. "You're saying more than that, Fargo," she said.

"I am," he admitted. "But that'll wait till later." He sent the pinto forward along the curving passage and eventually onto the high plain, moving along one edge where dense cottonwoods bordered the open land. He allowed himself a deep breath. It had gone so much better than he'd dared to hope, and it could have gone so much worse. He was grateful for that, but old questions demanded answers with new insistence. To go on without trying to uncover those answers was to invite new dangers. The spectre of death that had doggedly pursued could also lay in wait. He had to try to find answers, and he rode along the high plain until the sun began to dip to the horizon line. He found a place where the cottonwoods receded to form a half circle and waved the wagons into place when they finally rolled up.

He waited as darkness fell, gave everyone time to take their evening meal, and saw Alison had rolled her wagon to the very end of the group, a few yards off by itself. He had just finished his beef jerky when he watched Alison gather with Brenda, Pearl, and Ida Bluebell. They spoke far too quietly for him to hear, but the moonlight let him see there were no smiles. He rose and went to where Derek Hogath cleaned his tin plate. "Get everybody together for me," he said. "I've things that need saying."

He leaned against Hogath's wagon as the man hurried to the others, and it was but a few minutes when the silent figures gathered around him, their faces still wearing the marks of the day. "I'll start with Lieutenant Bowdon and Troop C. I'd guess they were dry-gulched and probably all killed," Fargo began. "Then the killers took their uniforms and horses. This time, instead of fake Cheyenne, they were fake cavalry troopers." He glanced at Alison, Brenda and Pearl behind her, and saw the pain in her eyes.

"It would have worked except for Fargo," Hogath put in. "As usual, he saw the things the rest of us didn't."

"I can't put much of this together, but I'm sure of two things," Fargo continued. "They were after whatever it was they didn't find in the attack on the other wagon train, and it has something to do with Fort Sanders. I can't say how or why, but I'm convinced it does. You folks and the other wagons were all on your way to the fort. Whatever it is they're after, somebody doesn't want it to reach the fort. They killed everyone on the other wagons to stop that. They were going to do the same to you." He paused and let his eyes travel over the faces in front of him, all reflecting new surprise and shock. "Any of you know a man named Kosta?" he asked.

"Not me," someone said.

"Me neither," another added, and a chorus of denials rose. "Why?" someone asked.

"I was told he's the key to everything else. He's done the hiring and the paying," Fargo said.

"Don't know any Kosta," someone said, and everyone murmured agreement.

"That still leaves one thing. Somebody's carrying whatever they're after," Fargo said.

The mutter rose at once, half shock, half protest. "I'm not carryin' anything anybody'd want to stop reaching the fort," a gray-bearded man said.

"Me neither," another said, followed by a rising crescendo of denial.

"Somebody is, and I'm going to find out," Fargo said, his voice hardening. "All the people in those first wagons deserve that much. So do the troopers that have been killed. And you folks, too, deserve knowing the truth. Come morning, I'm going to search every last thing you're carrying in your wagons."

"You don't even know what you're looking for," someone said.

"I'm hoping I'll know it when I find it," Fargo said.

"It's the only way we have to get answers," Derek Hogath said.

"If anyone has anything, or knows about anything, this is the time to speak up," Fargo said.

"I've nothing to hide. Do your searching come morning," the gray-bearded man said.

"That goes for all of us," a woman added.

"What if you don't find anything?" someone called out.

"You can go on, not knowing what might be waiting

for you, or you can turn back. It'll be your call," Fargo said.

"I can make that call now," Derek Hogath said. "We go on, no matter what. Everyone agree?"

"Damn right," the cry thundered as they returned to their wagons. He waited until they settled in and the half circle of wagons grew still, then took his bedroll and began to walk to the edge of the campsite. But as he passed Alison's wagon, the last in the half circle, he slowed. A small candle flickered inside the wagon and outlined the four figures, all sitting or standing in the cramped space. He could only catch an occasional sharp murmur of a voice raised, but there was no mistaking the angry tossing of heads, the sharp arm and hand gestures and the movements of confrontation.

He stepped deeper into the cottonwoods and continued to watch the shadow forms behind the canvas. The angry gestures went on until finally, Brenda swung down from the rear of the wagon followed by Pearl and Ida Bluebell. All three strode angrily to their wagons, and in moments the candle went out inside Alison's rig. Fargo put his bedroll down and stayed inside the trees, but he didn't stretch out. The shadowed confrontation inside the wagon pushed at him. Suddenly, all the answers and explanations Alison had once given him rose up again. They had left an unsatisfied feeling inside him then, but he'd put it aside and now it reasserted itself; the nurse and her three midwives who had to be at the opening of Fort Sanders, the need to be part of a new community that wouldn't need even one of them for damn near a year.

The explanation had bothered him then, and now it bothered him again, not unlike a toothache that went away, only to return with greater force. He was still turning thoughts when he saw the figure swing down from the rear of the wagon. Alison, a thin robe around her, carried some sort of flat leather pouch in one hand. In her other hand she carried a short-handled shovel. He watched her hurry into the trees, rose quickly, and, staying deeper in the thick foliage, he moved on silent cat's feet, paralleling her. She halted and dropped to her knees beside a tree some dozen feet from the wagon. Using the short-handled shovel, she began to dig at the base of the tree. He watched her dig a shallow hole and place the leather pouch inside it. Only when she started to put the dirt back into the hole did he step forward.

"You want to tell me what's in that?" he asked quietly.

Alison dropped the shovel in startled surprise as she looked up at him. He saw the gamut of expressions run through her face, shock, confusion, fright, embarrassment. He was glad to see pain included. It was somehow redeeming, a glimmer of evidence that beneath the lies and deceit she could feel.

5

"I don't figure to wait long," Fargo said. Alison looked at him for a drawn-out moment, and then her shoulders drooped, a silent gesture of defeat. She drew the leather pouch from the hole.

"How'd you know?" she asked.

"You keep your eyes open, you see things."

"Such as?"

"Shadows behind canvas. Motions that have meaning," he said, and she sighed deep from within. "I never did buy those reasons you gave. The shadows helped me remember that," he said. "Start with the truth, about yourself, about all of you. Start by dropping the midwife routine."

"It worked for everyone but you," she said.

"A lot of things work for other people," he said.

"Yes, I've come to know that," Alison said. "You're right, of course, about nobody being a midwife, though I am a nurse. We came here to let the world know the truth about General Billy Sanders, that murderer and fraud they want to name a fort after. The proof's all here, in the papers inside this pouch," she said, hugging the leather pouch to her.

"What kind of proof?" Fargo queried.

"Come to the wagon," she said, then rose, and he followed her as she kept the pouch clutched to her breasts. Inside the wagon she lighted the small candle and gestured to the narrow cot. Fargo sat on the edge, and she folded herself on the floor of the wagon in front of him. She shrugged her robe off, and he watched how beautifully the silk nightdress clung to her, outlining her full breasts as if it were hardly there at all. "I guess the best place to start is with General Sanders," she said.

"Why not?" Fargo agreed.

"The general was a liar, a fraud, and a disgrace to the uniform he wore. They can't name a fort after him. It must be stopped. The truth about him must come out," Alison said, her voice gathering determination.

"And you've come to do that, with Pearl, Brenda, and Ida?"

"Yes," she said, hissing the word. "We've reasons, each of us. Let's start with mine. My father was Captain Alistair Carter, U.S. Cavalry. Sanders was a colonel then. But Sanders set out to make himself a general, and he killed my father in the process, deliberately and purposefully. There were others he killed, too."

"Those are strong words, girl," Fargo said.

"And true, every one of them. Sanders was never any good. I came to find that out about him. He was a man without honor, without decency. He schemed and planned his way to becoming a general. The key to it all was his glowing report of the very large and very superior force of Pawnee he destroyed. His report set down all the details of the action. It made wonderful reading, and he documented it by having fifty pine box sealed caskets shipped by wagon as proof. There were three newspaper reporters at the army depot who saw the caskets and watched the burial. They sent all kinds of dispatches that confirmed his report to headquarters. Unknowingly, they aided in his lies."

"You saying he didn't destroy a big Pawnee force? He didn't conduct an action against an Indian force?"

"Oh, he conducted an action against the Indians. He raided a camp of Poncas, mostly women, children, and old men. He slaughtered almost all of them. Those were the great Pawnee warriors he had shipped and buried. Between his report and the dispatches of the newspapermen, headquarters swallowed every word of it. He was the latest hero, and they made him a general."

"The troopers he commanded, they knew they'd slaughtered women and children. They knew it was no great victory. Nobody spoke up?" Fargo questioned.

"Almost nobody. You know the army. A private isn't going to speak out against his commander. And Sanders had planned everything so cleverly. He gave every one of his troopers a promotion and a medal for their bravery. With a promotion and added pay, they stayed quiet."

"You said *almost* nobody spoke up," Fargo reminded her.

"My father was one of the few who did. He said he was going to tell the truth about what happened. Of course, Sanders couldn't permit that. He knew that the chief of the Poncas, normally fairly peaceable, looked to revenge the slaughter of almost his entire tribe of women and children. He lay back with his remaining braves, waiting for a chance to strike. Sanders gave him that chance. He sent my father out on patrol with only eight troopers. He told my father that the Poncas had been seen running south. Sending a patrol out with false information, knowing death lay in wait, is murder, nothing else but murder. The Ponca chief struck and killed everyone except one trooper who managed to escape. General Sanders silenced the one man who was going to speak out against him, to tell the truth about him."

"So you decided to come here and avenge your father's murder by setting the record straight," Fargo said.

"Yes, but not just *his* murder. I want to avenge the killing of everyone that General Billy Sanders so cleverly engineered to make himself a general. I want to stop the army from naming a fort after this lying, cheating, murdering fraud."

"You said you had proof in that pouch. What kind of proof?" Fargo questioned.

"When Sanders deliberately sent my father to his death, he didn't know that my father had written me a letter detailing the truth about what Sanders had done, exposing him for the lying, ambitious bastard that he was. I have that letter in this pouch. I told you that one man escaped the Ponca revenge attack. He was trooper Paul Jackson, Brenda's younger brother." She paused, and Fargo felt his brows lift. "Paul Jackson escaped with his life, but he was a broken man. He was afraid to go back to Sanders, afraid the general would plan another attempt on his life, afraid to trust anybody. He ran and wound up at Brenda's. Little by little she helped him gather himself. She got him to write down everything that had happened, starting with Sanders's massacre of the Ponca women and children. I have that testimony in the pouch, too. Paul is across the border now, still hiding."

"And Pearl?" Fargo asked.

"Pearl was engaged to one of the troopers Sanders sent to his death. He was with her the night before they went out. He told her of Sanders's lie about how the Ponca were running south. He told her they were all afraid the Ponca were out there waiting for revenge. I have everything he told Pearl in the pouch, three documented indictments of Sanders. And one more," Alison added.

"Ida Bluebell," Fargo said.

"She's a Ponca. She was in the Ponca camp when Sanders attacked. She managed to get away, the only one who did. She ran, terrified, for days and days until finally, exhausted and unconscious, she was found by Abel and Harriet Temple. Harriet and Abel ran a missionary school and happened to be friends of mine. That's where I met Ida. They took her in, taught her English, and in time she confirmed everything my father had written me. I decided to get together with Brenda, Pearl, and Ida and tell the truth about General Billy Sanders."

Fargo leaned back and regarded Alison in the last of the flickering candlelight and believed her thoroughly, no arrogance left in her face, no stiff masks. "This explains away that phony midwife routine and why you're carrying so little in your wagons. You've no intention of settling in here. But why go to all this trouble and come way out here? If you've all this proof, why didn't you go to Washington and the army Board of Review?"

The anger came into Alison's face again. "We tried that," she spit out derisively. "We went to Washington. I had to put down the reasons why we wanted a hearing. I expected that would be kept confidential. I was too trusting. Word got out, and strange men showed up. They tried to kidnap me. They tried to get to Brenda and Pearl, too. We had Ida hidden away. We had to run for our lives. Apparently, Sanders had friends in high places."

"Sanders was still alive then. I can understand somebody getting word to him and his taking steps, calling in favors. But he died over a year ago," Fargo said.

"And it didn't stop. So when we heard that the army was going to name a new fort after him with a big dedication ceremony, we decided to be here and present everything we had to the officials. We'd get around the army and its damn spiderweb of connections. I hear the secretary of the army will be there, General Hawkins, the chief of staff, Senator Connolly representing the President, and a lot of others. We'll just give them the evidence we have and nobody can stop us there."

"Only somebody is trying to stop you, all the way out here," Fargo said.

"I know," Alison said, pain sweeping into her eyes. "I'm so sick about those poor people on the other wagon train. They died for nothing."

"Somebody's real serious about this. Word's got out there's going to be an attempt to reach the officials at the dedication, but they don't know who's going to carry it. That's why they've been out to kill anybody trying to reach the fort. But the whole thing still makes no damn sense. Sanders is dead. Why would anyone be trying to protect his name?"

"I don't know, but in snooping around, I learned that some thirty-five years ago he had a long-running affair with a rich woman in Washington. I heard she went on to marry a United States senator, but that's all I know," Alison said.

"Then she wouldn't have any reason to protect Sanders's name. That makes no damn sense, either. It's somebody who wants to keep him from being exposed, to protect his name and his image. Somebody knows what a bastard he was and doesn't want the world to know it," Fargo said, and Alison shrugged helplessly as he peered at her. "What was the argument between you and the other girls?" he asked.

She looked at him with embarrassment. "They wanted me to tell you about everything, to trust you," she said.

"But you couldn't manage that."

"Not after everything that's happened," she said, defensive at once. "I wanted to, especially after you saved my neck with that rattler. But you were always a little suspicious. I couldn't be sure what that meant. I was afraid to trust you, to trust anybody, especially after Washington."

"And now?" he pushed at her.

"It doesn't seem I've any choice left," she said. "And I'm too tired not to trust anymore. I guess you've got to take a chance on somebody." She leaned forward, and the tops of her breasts swelled over the edge of the nightdress as she came to him, her mouth finding his, a lingering, sweet touch, and then she drew back.

"No more watchdog?" he murmured.

"I didn't say that," Alison answered quickly. "But for different reasons."

"Only that was always part of it." He laughed, and she looked away.

"Now what?" she asked.

"I don't like the idea of your going on to the fort without some idea what they may have waiting as you get

87

near. They've been pretty ruthless up to now. I don't see them suddenly backing off."

"We've come this far. We're not backing off, either. We're all agreed on that," Alison said.

"We need some help. I'm going to go back and see Major Foster. I've enough to make him listen to me now. He won't want trouble at the dedication. Taking command of the fort is a big thing with him," Fargo said. "I'll find a place for the wagons to wait till I get back."

"It's time to be honest with the others," Alison said. "They might refuse to have us along. I wouldn't blame them. We're a liability."

"You owe them that call," Fargo agreed, and she nodded resignedly. He rose, and she clung to him for a moment longer, all warm softness under the thin silk. "We'll talk more come morning," he said and swung from the wagon. He had walked halfway to where he'd left his bedroll when he saw Brenda step from the shadows.

"I couldn't sleep. I got up and saw you go into Alison's wagon with her. She told you everything?" Brenda asked.

"Yes," he said.

"You tell her everything?" Brenda asked further, a tiny smile coming to her slightly pudgy face.

"Didn't see any need for that. It wasn't general confession time," Fargo said.

"Good," Brenda said. "Alison's more than a little interested in you."

"She tell you that?"

"No, but she didn't have to. We all see it, and we don't want to hurt her. She's brought us all together in this. She's been the force that got us to do what we all felt should be done about Sanders. Without her we'd never have come this far."

"So you're feeling protective about her."

"Guess so."

Fargo slid a smile at Brenda. "It's easy to be generous when you've already had your cake," he commented.

"Guess so." She laughed. "But I'll be around, just in case." She turned and hurried away, and Fargo found his bedroll and stretched out. He slept at once and woke with the new day, washed, and dressed, then found Alison facing the others as they took breakfast, Pearl, Brenda, and Ida beside her.

"There'll be no need to search your wagons," she said. "I'm here to tell you what I told Fargo late last night." She spoke quickly, leaving out some of the details she'd told about in the wagon as Fargo watched. "We'll go on our own if that's what you decide, and we'll understand. None of this is your fight, except in the most general way," she finished.

Derek Hogath spoke for the others. "I don't like casting anyone out. I'd like to hear what Fargo has to say," he said.

"I'm going to try and get help. Meanwhile, I can say this. Whoever's behind this doesn't know who has what they want. That's why they're out to kill everyone. You can't divorce yourselves from these young women. They won't let you. Their orders are to take no chances," Fargo said.

"Maybe we put an end to them," someone said.

"You ready to take that chance?" Fargo tossed back, and there was only silence as his answer. "Maybe we won't have to worry about that when I get back. Meanwhile, let's roll." He climbed onto the pinto and led the way north, sweeping the terrain as he rode ahead, finally coming upon an almost perfect spot, a steep draw covered by a thick growth of red cedar. It ended against a small lake, and he brought the wagons in and saw that each pulled up under a canopy of the dense foliage. "You'll stay here till I get back. Keep out of sight by day. You can catch fresh fish in the lake at night. Keep your cook fires small to play safe, though this draw makes a damn good hideaway. I'll be back as soon as I can, with a company of troopers, I hope," he said.

Alison came to his side, Brenda, Pearl, and Ida looking on. "Good luck from all of us," she said.

"If you're of a mind to pray, this might be a good time," he said and sent the Ovaro out of the draw at a fast trot. He retraced steps, and it was midafternoon when he pulled to a halt as he moved across a narrow stretch of flat land. An odor rose up to fill the air, a foul blanket. His lips pulled taut. He knew that odor. Once you smelled it, you never forgot, and he'd smelled it all too often and had never grown used to it, the cloying, strange acridness of it, somehow both sour and sweet and altogether sickening, the odor of death.

He came to a dip in the land and saw the dozen figures strewn along the ground, stripped to their underwear by men, stripped to their flesh by beast and worm. He put a kerchief over his face as he threaded his way through the terrible scene, peering down, counting, trying to see if he could still recognize an earnest, young face. But he couldn't, and he was about to climb out of the dip of land when he reined to a halt. A set of footprints led away from the bodies, a single, lone set of prints. He turned the pinto and followed after the footprints, saw them form an erratic pattern, waver from side to side, drag across the ground, suddenly stop, and the grass flatten out in front of them. But they went on again, unsteady, almost aimless, and he felt a surge of hope flare within. Someone had staggered away from the killing scene. He followed the footprints, saw them stop again, and examined the flattened area of grass. The man had lain here, probably for the night, the footprints visible again a dozen feet on. Fargo followed till the day ended and the night made picking up the prints an impossibility.

He set out his bedroll and slept until the dawn came when he dressed and again pursued the prints. They were less erratic now, moving in a straighter line, and he paused from time to time to dismount and go over the prints with his fingers, seeing with touch and feel, reading the delicate messages in a blade of grass, a crust of earth. By midday he knew the man was not far ahead, and he saw where he'd stopped at a stream to drink. But he was growing very tired, the footsteps dragging, and it was when Fargo crested a low rise that he saw the figure lying on the ground. He sent the pinto into a canter, and the figure pushed up on one elbow, then struggled to its feet and waved. Fargo came to a halt and looked down at Tom Bowdon, his face suddenly grown older, his underwear stained with blood and dirt, his eyes still filled with horror and pain.

"Jesus, Fargo. Oh, God, how'd you find me?" the lieutenant asked.

"That was the easy part," Fargo said. "How'd you stay alive?"

"I'd just raised my rifle when the bullet hit me, strong enough to knock me off my horse and draw blood. They must've thought I was dead. I was unconscious and bleeding. But the bullet had hit my carbine, which took most of its force. When I woke up, everyone was dead, all our uniforms taken. They never gave us a chance. They stopped us to ask directions and just opened fire, point-blank," the lieutenant said.

"They were going to massacre everybody in the wagons," Fargo said. "We turned it around. They're all dead."

"Serves them right," Bowdon said. "Where are you going now?"

"Same place you are, to see Major Foster," Fargo said, reached down and gripped Bowdon's hand, and pulled him up behind him on the Ovaro. "Think you can ride the rest of the way?"

"I'll ride," the lieutenant said grimly, though Fargo heard him wince in pain as he came onto the horse. Fargo sent the pinto forward at a slow trot. "I think the major will pay attention now," Fargo said.

"Can you put this all together?" Bowdon asked.

"No, but I know some of it, enough to get him to listen," Fargo said and increased the pinto's pace only to realize he had to slow as he felt Bowdon clinging with pain-racked desperation.

"Sorry," the younger man said when Fargo stopped to let him rest. "My whole chest hurts. That bullet didn't kill me, but it bruised my breastbone."

"No apologies. We'll get there tonight after dark," Fargo said and sent the Ovaro forward at a walk. He kept a steady but slow pace and watched the day slide into evening, then the black of night. But he had spotted enough natural marks to know they were within hours of Dennison. The moon had risen high in the sky when he

92

finally rode the horse through the dark, still houses of the town, and the darkened army stockade loomed up in front of him. Two sentries straightened up at the gate, their eyes widening as Bowdon slid to the ground and clung to Fargo's arm to avoid collapsing.

"Jesus," one of the sentries said.

"Get the doc," Fargo said, and one of the sentries rushed away while the other hurried to put one arm under Bowdon. Fargo swung from the saddle and helped support the lieutenant until the other sentry returned with a gray-haired man tying a bathrobe around him.

"Into the infirmary with him," the company doctor ordered the two soldiers and then turned to Fargo. "What happened?" he asked.

"Troop C was ambushed. He's the only one left," Fargo said.

"Indians, of course," the doctor said.

"No, a band of dry-gulchers. The lieutenant will tell you," Fargo said, and the doctor hurried into the compound after his patient. Fargo started to cross the compound to the major's quarters when a soldier came out of the darkness, carbine in hand. "Have to see the major," Fargo said.

"Not till morning," the soldier said.

"It's important," Fargo tried.

"Strict orders. He's not to be disturbed for anything, not till morning," the soldier said. His face said he wasn't about to be convinced otherwise, so Fargo walked from the compound. A few hours wouldn't make all that much difference, he told himself as he led the Ovaro into a line of hackberry that ran just behind the rear of the compound. He set out his bedroll, undressed, and let sleep take charge, waking only when the new day's sun warmed the land. He washed with his canteen water, dressed, and was on his way to the major's quarters when he met the doctor.

"He's almost good as new," the doctor said without waiting for his query. "Another day will do it. Youth is a great help to the body." Fargo nodded and walked on to where the door to the major's quarters hung open. He entered, and Major Foster stood up behind his desk, the man's brisk bantam-cock arrogance still very much part of him.

"Been expecting you, Fargo," Major Foster said. "I already saw Lieutenant Bowdon. He told me about the ambush. He said you know more about it than he does."

"The attack, and the other one on the wagons, they were all to stop something from reaching Fort Sanders," Fargo said.

"Something?" The major frowned.

"Information, proof, facts four young women are bringing," Fargo said.

"To tell what?"

"To tell the truth about the late General Billy Sanders, to prove that he was a murderer, a liar, and a disgrace to his uniform," Fargo said.

"That's a mighty strong accusation," Major Foster said.

"They've proof. But they have to get it to the fort and the officials who are going to be there for the dedication. I need you to send a company to see that they get there alive," Fargo said.

"I can't do that. I've just enough men to escort the official party and keep a garrison here," Foster said. "Where are these young women now?"

"I've got them hidden away for now, along with the rest of the new settlers," Fargo said.

Major Foster's lips pursed in thought as he peered at Fargo. "The lieutenant says you people wiped out the men who attacked Troop C. Maybe you did them in once and for all with that."

"And maybe I didn't. That's a chance I don't want to take. I need a company of troops. The doc says Lieutenant Bowdon will be fit to ride tomorrow," Fargo said.

"I'm going to need him here, especially now that I'm short Troop C," Foster said. "Sending a company of men with you is out of the question. I'm expecting the official party in a day or two. But perhaps I can come up with something. Let me think further about this. Stop by later today."

"Is that all?" Fargo questioned. "I thought you'd be curious about the charges against General Sanders."

Foster fastened him with a hard and arrogant glance. "I'll wait till the charges are properly brought. I'm not interested in hearing the good name of an officer of the United States Cavalry dragged through the mud anymore than I need to," he said. "You just stop by later." Fargo turned away at the icy dismissal and strode from the room.

Outside, he seethed inwardly, though he realized he had no cause to be surprised. The officer code of the army. It protected its own, perpetuated by a select little club that cared more about their privileges than truth. He could deplore it, but he couldn't ignore it. Except for a few strong, independent men, it was part of the system, and it left a bad taste in his mouth whenever he came onto it. Nevertheless, he had no choice but to wait to see what Foster would decide to do, so he strolled from the compound and surprised Cindy at the store. She was in his arms at once. "You're back," she murmured.

"Not for long," he said.

"Have we time to go to the cabin?" she asked.

"God, I wish we did," he said, holding her soft warmth. "Next visit, I promise."

"How about coffee and biscuits?" she asked with the unflappable realism that was part of her. He nodded and hungrily breakfasted with her as she used a small hearth behind the store. Her lips clung to his when he finally left as the afternoon grew long. Cindy had seen to it that the visit hadn't been entirely platonic, and he left wishing he could stay. As he reached the compound, he was surprised to see Tom Bowdon in uniform, though with the top buttons undone.

"You make a quick recovery, Lieutenant," Fargo said.

"Thanks to you. I was getting real weak when you found me. Worse, I was pretty thoroughly lost. I'd never have made it back," Bowdon said.

"I haven't gotten what I wanted from the major," Fargo said.

"He's not about to let your agenda interfere with his, and his is getting the dignitaries to the fort," the lieutenant said.

"I hoped you might put in a good word," Fargo said.

"I tried. I was told he didn't need advice from junior officers," Bowdon said, and Fargo grunted inwardly. There was more acceptance than annoyance in Bowdon's voice. The army instilled obedience in its young officers.

"Thanks for trying," Fargo said and hurried to the

major's quarters as dusk began to drift across the office.

"Been giving this a lot of thought," Foster said. "Here's what you're going to do. You go back to your people and wait three days after you get there. Then you move on to the fort just as you normally would. I'll be there by the time you arrive, so you'll have protection when you meet the official party."

"That the best you can do?" Fargo questioned.

"Yes, but it'll be the best thing for everybody. That'll let me have the official party in place at the fort. That is who these young women want to see, isn't it?" Foster said, and Fargo nodded. "If you follow exactly what I've laid out for you, things will go fine. But the timing is going to be vital. If you get to the fort too early, there might be another attack on the wagons, which you're afraid of now. The dedication is going to be short, so if you get to the fort too late, the official party may have left and those young woman won't get a chance at a meeting. That's why it's important you follow the timetable I've laid out." He halted, his stare made of cold arrogance.

"You don't leave me much choice," Fargo said.

"Circumstances dictate things," Foster said, and Fargo turned and strode from the room. Dismissal was not just the major's prerogative, he muttered, hurrying outside. Night had come to blanket the land as he led the Ovaro from the compound. He had gone into the hackberry at the rear of the depot when he caught the movement to his right and halted at once. A man led two horses along the edge of the trees, and as he moved closer, Fargo recognized the thin, reedy figure with the army-issue boots and the Indian shawl around his shoulders. Thin Tree, the major's scout, Fargo grunted and watched the man lead the two horses deeper into the trees and come to a halt. The scout was plainly waiting for someone. He wouldn't wait alone, Fargo thought and continued to stroke the Ovaro to keep the horse quiet.

Fargo's gaze traveled across the darkness, and he guessed perhaps a half hour had passed when he saw a figure suddenly appear from the rear of the compound. The man wore a hat pulled low, with a wide brim, and a jacket and Levi's, but there was no mistaking the quick steps of the bantam-rooster stride. A frown dug into Fargo's brow as Major Foster hurried into the trees, climbed onto the second horse, and both men set off at a fast canter. Fargo swung onto his horse and followed, staying far back. That gave him no problem as the major and his scout were intent on speed, not silence. They swung east almost at once, then north, riding hard, and Fargo continued to keep far back as he followed. They had crossed into Dakota territory before the moon reached the midnight sky, and they kept their hard pace, stopping only once to rest the horses.

They concentrated on making time, riding over open flat land as much as they could, and Fargo kept plenty of distance behind, following more by sound than sight. The moon had begun to dip toward the horizon, and they had covered plenty of ground in their driving pace, when the two riders turned into a forest of ironwood. Fargo went in after them, drawing closer when he was inside the heavy forest, and suddenly he smelled wood smoke. He slowed, and he could see the dark forms of the two riders ahead of him, and then, moments after, the camp came into view. He saw the tipis first, a half dozen of them, almost certain at once from the three-pole construction of the tents. His certainty was verified when he drew close enough to see the Cheyenne markings decorating the outer canvas of each tipi. He halted as he saw the major and Thin Tree ride into the camp where a double line of near-naked bucks waited.

Dismounting, he tethered the pinto to a low branch and went closer on foot, moving on silent footsteps, though all concentration seemed to be on the new arrivals in the camp. Halting alongside the brown, scaly bark of a thick ironwood, he saw the flap open on the nearest tipi and a figure step out. The man was tall, muscular, wearing deerskin britches, a beaded armband, and the two golden eagle feathers in the crown of his thick, bear-greased hair that marked him as a chief. Foster and the scout dismounted, and Fargo saw the chief's broad-featured face watch both with a stony, impassive expression. Thin Tree quickly spoke in Algonkian to the tall figure. "This is the man I came to you about. He is called Foster," the scout said.

"The one who asks to speak to Strong Wing, chief of the Cheyenne," the tall figure said.

"Yes. He brings an offer to the great chief," Thin Tree said, and Fargo heard the nervousness in his voice.

"What kind of offer?" the Cheyenne asked.

The scout looked at Foster, who spoke at once. "I can help the chief wipe out the bluecoats and the new fort," Foster said, and the scout translated.

The Cheyenne chief's stone-faced expression did not change. He took his eyes from Foster and turned them on the scout. "Why does he bring me this offer?" Strong Wing asked, and Fargo caught the mixture of suspicion and disdain in his voice.

"Like the Cheyenne, he wants no new bluecoat fort," Thin Tree said.

"Why?" the Indian snapped.

"They will not let him sell many things. They will be bad for him, just as they will be for the Cheyenne. He wants them gone, all killed, the fort burned down," Thin Tree said, and Fargo felt a frown digging deep into his brow. "But he cannot do this by himself. That is why he comes to the Cheyenne."

The Cheyenne chief's black eyes fastened on the major, but he spoke to Thin Tree. "What can he tell the Cheyenne?" the chief asked.

"He knows what the bluecoats will do. He can tell Strong Wing when and how to wipe out the new fort," Thin Tree said as Foster stood by.

The Cheyenne chief was silent for a moment, but finally he nodded. "We will talk in the tipi," he said, and Fargo cursed silently as Foster and the scout followed the Indian into the tent. Frustration swept through Fargo, and he felt his fists clenching. He didn't dare crawl any closer to the tipi and probably couldn't hear through the thick canvas if he did. The meaning of what he'd seen and heard defied explanation. Only the facts formed a picture that drenched him in shock. Foster had come to enlist the Cheyenne in an attack on the fort, a last elaborate attempt to stop Alison's message from reaching official ears. But why? The question flew against him as a caged eagle flies against its bars. Was it a sick, twisted exercise in army loyalty? Fargo rejected the thought at once. It wasn't enough, not nearly enough. There had to be more, something else. It didn't make any damn sense. It defied logic and went against all understanding. Even the fact that Foster was here with the Cheyenne defied understanding.

Fargo sank onto one knee and hoped he wasn't still waiting there when the sun came up.

6

More often than not, waiting was a tedious business when time dragged with maddening slowness. But this night Fargo was all too aware of how time could hurry. He marshaled the few facts that he had and went over each one again to see if they would somehow explain the unanswered. The major was behind all the disguised attacks that had taken place. He had caused one entire troop of his own men to be slaughtered, and now he was making a devil's bargain with the Cheyenne. All was designed to keep Alison's message from being heard. This last effort now going on inside the tipi depended on all the pieces coming together at the right time. This was the most precarious of all his efforts and the last chance left to him.

He had already set some of those pieces in motion, Fargo realized now. Those were the detailed instructions Foster had given him, all part of the plan he was fashioning in this last desperate effort. Those were the hard facts he now had, Fargo thought, but they failed to provide the real answers. Why? What did it all mean? One more thing kept surfacing, the icy ruthlessness of Major Elmont Foster. But what fed this savage loyalty? What made the reputation and name of General Billy Sanders so sacred to him? Had Major Foster somehow been involved in the massacre Alison wanted to expose? Or perhaps in others? Was he afraid that exposing Sanders would lead to revelations about him? Self-protection? That was a powerful motive that often masks itself as loyalty. Angrily, Fargo pushed aside the questions that spun through his head. He didn't want more questions. He wanted answers, and they still danced out of reach.

Suddenly, he felt himself grow cold. It had only been a soft breeze, but it had sent a chill through him. A soft breeze, a morning breeze. He stood up, aware of the subtle change in the forest, the blackness that was suddenly less black. Dawn was sliding its way into the forest, and he knew how quickly dawn could come. In only a few minutes the forest would be light enough for the Cheyenne braves in the camp to see through the trees. If they didn't spot him, chances were that Thin Tree would when he left with the major. Fargo moved silently away in the very beginning of the dawn, back to where he'd left the Ovaro, and he led the horse to the edge of the ironwoods. He found a spot behind two thick old trees and waited.

Almost an hour passed when he saw Foster and the scout pass through the trees and out into the open land in the new sun. They rode hard, and Fargo knew the devil's bargain had been sealed. But what was it? What had the major convinced the Cheyenne chief to do? He had to find out, Fargo told himself as he let the two men ride out of sight before he followed their fresh tracks. The sun moved across the sky, and it was noon before he neared where they had stopped to bed down in a clump of shadbush. Their need to rest was real enough. They had ridden most of the night. But the major had another reason, Fargo realized. He didn't want to return to the compound till after dark. Fargo felt tiredness pulling at him also and chose a low ridge of thick wild teasel, some of the weedy brush eight feet high. He sank down in its pale lavender and delicate green and let himself sleep as the pinto wandered in a nearby clump of blue-grass.

But like the mountain lion, he let only a part of himself sleep and woke at once, hours later, as a faint sound came to his ears. He sat up and listened to the distant sound of hoofbeats moving across the ground at a fast canter. Instantly awake, he swung onto the pinto and followed the tracks in the last light of the day. When night came, he again let hearing replace seeing as he stayed on the trail of the two riders. Through the night he kept the dogged pursuit. The moon had crossed the midnight sky when the dark shapes of the houses of Dennison came into sight. He spurred the Ovaro on, veered right, and passed Foster and the scout. He had halted inside the hackberry at the rear of the compound when the major appeared, on foot, hurrying along the rear fence of the compound, hat pulled low.

Fargo watched as the major went almost to the last corner of the compound and carefully slipped through a loose post in the fence. Fargo snorted as another little piece of the puzzle took shape. The major plainly covered his absence from the base by leaving strict orders he was not to be disturbed for anything. It was not the first time he had slipped away for a day, Fargo was certain. Fargo turned the horse and slowly rode back through the hackberry to the front of the compound, then climbed up a slope into the low, tree-covered hills and found a spot hidden away. He dismounted, set out his bedroll, and lay down for a good night's sleep. When day came, he sat up and was pleased with the spot he'd chosen. It let him stay hidden, yet he could see down to the compound below and the land surrounding it. He also found a tiny brook nearby and an arbor of blueberries that let him leisurely breakfast as he peered down on the scene below.

A slow but steady flow of horses and wagons, mostly farm wagons and surreys, passed near the compound, a few entering, and he watched a platoon of troopers at drill. It was midmorning when he saw the flurry of activity below, and then the two big Concord coaches rolled into the compound, each pulled by a six-horse team. He could only glimpse a little of the activity after they pulled into the compound, but he heard the trumpeter sound a military fanfare. The official party had arrived. Fargo sat back as he estimated they'd take an hour or two to freshen up and eat before leaving for the last leg of their trip to the fort. As the time went on, he caught sight of two or three well-dressed men as they wandered from inside the compound, and it was almost two hours later when he saw the two big Concords wheeled to the gate.

The dignitaries climbed into the heavy coaches, a driver and brakeman on each. Moments after, the military escort rode from the compound led by Major Foster. Fargo found himself leaning forward, a furrow crossing his brow. He counted only twelve troopers as they formed a line on each side of the coaches. He stared, surprise whirling inside him. Twelve troopers, thirteen with the major, fourteen with the scout, Thin Tree, that rode a few yards ahead of the major. It didn't make any damn sense unless he was certain the Cheyenne wouldn't attack. But if that were so, what did that mean? Fargo continued to frown after the two big Concords as they rolled out of sight. He sat back, and Foster's instructions to him swam into his mind. He went over them again, but they offered no insights into the strange spectacle of only twelve troopers accompanying the official party. But he was certain of one thing. Foster had a reason. It was all part of his plan, whatever that was, and Fargo knew he needed more pieces to figure that out.

He sat back, cursing softly, very aware that he was pushing into the all-important element of time. But he forced himself to stay with the plan he had set out for himself. He watched a squad engage in a drill below as the remainder of the day drew to a close and night descended. He waited another hour and then slowly led the Ovaro down the slope, tethering the horse to a branch when he neared the edge of the trees. The compound gate closed, and dark silence took over as Fargo moved on foot along the edge of the hackberry until he was across from the rear fence. Darting into the open, he flattened himself against the tall thick poles that formed the compound fence, pressed each as he moved along. He had almost reached the rear corner when he felt the pole move at his pressure. It moved enough to let him slide his way into the compound where he halted and let his eyes sweep the darkness. Nothing moved, no sentries patrolled, and Fargo glided forward on silent steps.

He reached the buildings inside the compound, saw the two sentries at the gate as he crept to the major's quarters, and carefully pushed the door open just wide enough for him to slip inside. A faint ray of moonlight let him find the kerosene lamp, and he turned it on at its very lowest, just enough to let him see the interior of the quarters a few feet from where he stood. He set the lamp on the floor as he began to go through every drawer of the major's desk. His lips were tight as he found nothing but sheafs of reports, requisitions, and ordinary army paperwork. He looked inside a half-empty box of long, thin, phosphorous-tipped lucifers, found nothing but the matches and took the lamp with him into the adjoining room. An army cot and a wooden clothes closet took up one side of the room, two trunks the other side. Fargo set the lamp on the floor again as he opened the first trunk and began to search through it.

It revealed nothing but clothes, two holsters, and a pair of six-shot, single-action New Model Army pistols with rounded barrel and trigger guards. He closed the trunk and opened the next one, found the top part of the contents made of bedding linen. But he felt a stab of excitement when he lifted all the linen out and saw the two albums and photos in ornate frames. He examined the pictures in the albums, all daguerreotypes of faded sepia. Three were of a woman and three of a child, a young boy Fargo guessed to be eight or ten years old. He stared at the pictures, examined each carefully, and took in the initials on the back of each. He put them aside and picked up a document that lay under the pictures. It was, he quickly saw, a birth certificate in the ornate, scrolled style of the period and imprinted with an official seal. At the bottom there were two signatures, one over the title *Physician,* the other over the words *Records Clerk—City of Washington.* But in the center, at the place for the name of the person registered, there was nothing, the space left blank. There was another piece of paper under the certificate, and Fargo looked at it to find it was an exact duplicate, again with the seal, physician's signature, and records clerk signature at the bottom but the name left blank at the center.

As he stared at the two certificates, identical in every respect, their real meaning took shape. They were fraudulent, carefully crafted fakes, ready and waiting for whatever name was to be filled in. There was no other explanation for two birth certificates signed and countersigned with the vital name left blank. Another thought leaped to his mind as he stared at them. There had probably been a third that had the name filled in and used. These two were backups in case they'd been needed. But what were they doing in Elmont Foster's trunk? The question danced wildly inside him as he read the next document at the bottom of the trunk. This turned out to be admission papers to the Military Academy at West Point. Fargo read through the formal admission papers and paused at the line near the bottom that said: *Approved by Colonel Billy Sanders, USA.* Fargo's lips pursed as he stared at the signature.

So Sanders had approved Foster's admission to the academy. That hardly justified the kind of ruthless loyalty Foster was engaged in. Fargo picked up the last piece of paper in the trunk and saw it was also on official army stationery, a recommendation of Foster's promotion to major. His eyes held on the signature at the bottom, *General Billy Sanders.* Fargo's lips formed a thin line as he stared at the two documents. Sanders had plainly been the major's mentor, but the two documents taken together weren't enough to explain Foster's acts. That was still carrying loyalty and gratitude to monstrous lengths. There had to be more behind it, but there was nothing more in the trunk, so he returned to examining again everything he'd found.

He let thoughts chase themselves through his mind at will, freely associate with each other, explore their own possible conclusions. His mind wandered down avenues of speculation, and he found himself staring again and again at the daguerreotypes of the young boy. He mused in silence, thoughts churning, when suddenly he felt the muscles of his jaw grow tight. Pieces began to come together, not all of them yet, but enough to add new depths to old crimes, enough to disturb the shadows of old skeletons. He rose and put everything back into the trunk except one of the daguerreotypes, which he slid into his pocket. Outside, the night was edging to an end, and he left the compound the way he'd entered, through the loose section of the rear gate. He darted into the hackberry, led the Ovaro up the slope, and managed to get in a few hours of sleep before morning dawned.

After he washed and dressed at the little stream, he wandered down to the compound and frowned when he saw Tom Bowdon watching over the entire company as the men groomed and curried their mounts and went over their gear. The lieutenant saw him approach, and surprise flooded his face. "Thought you'd left, Fargo," Bowdon said.

"I'm on my way. Looks like you're getting all shined up and ready to sparkle," Fargo said.

"I'll be taking the entire company to Fort Sanders," Bowdon said, and Fargo's eyes lifted.

"The entire company?"

"In full battle gear. The major's orders. He gave me special instructions to wait a full day and then proceed to the fort," Bowdon said.

Fargo frowned as he silently counted. "That'd bring you to the fort in three days," he concluded.

"That's how I figure it, given a good ride with no problems," Bowdon agreed.

Thoughts tumbled through Fargo's mind. Foster had left yesterday with but twelve troopers, yet he arranged to have the entire company follow three days later. And before he'd given those orders, he'd met with the Cheyenne. Fargo's thoughts continued to race as he swore under his breath. If he was right, the devil's bargain inside the tipi had suddenly become clear, and another piece of the final picture fell into place. If he was right, Fargo reminded himself as he cursed Elmont Foster's desperately devious cleverness. But there was only one way to find out if he was right, he realized, and he turned and climbed onto the Ovaro.

"Good luck, Lieutenant. Maybe I'll see you soon," he said and sent the horse into a gallop. Trying to explain it all to the lieutenant was out of the question. He would never accept the enormity of it. There was still too much army in him, all those principles and traditions of respect and integrity that had taken all those years of training to instill in him. His own sense of honor and loyalty would never permit it, not without the proof that couldn't be denied. But Fargo knew he hadn't that kind of proof to offer, not yet. He had only words, the pieces of a puzzle that still needed finishing, and that wouldn't be enough. He had to finish the picture, see it through and hope he was right about the last devil's bargain. He threw a grim snort into the wind since he knew that if he had guessed wrong he would have made his last guess. Yet he did not slow the pinto's thundering hooves. It was past time for slowing. Time was vital, more than ever now, and he turned the horse northeast and rode hard, pausing only once to let the horse drink at a pond.

The day was nearing an end when he reached the Dakota territory, but he plunged on as night descended. The moon came up to let him glimpse the natural markers that were printed into his mind, and he watched the silver sphere slowly trace its way across the deep blue velvet of the night sky. The moon had almost touched the horizon when he saw the heavy stand of ironwood that marked the place of the Cheyenne camp. He slowed, entered the forest, and left the Ovaro only a dozen yards from the camp and went the rest of the way on foot. The camp was a silent, sleeping place, the dark outlines of the tipis rising into the air. He saw the first glimmer of dawn as he stepped into the camp, moving silently on the balls of his feet to halt just outside the chief's tipi. Folding himself cross-legged on the ground, he sat down and waited, aware that the figures asleep on the ground nearby wouldn't wake until the sun sifted through the trees.

They felt secure, strong, and Fargo stayed unmoving as the new sun began to spread its yellow warmth across the camp. But he could distinguish the sleeping Cheyenne braves only a dozen feet away and felt surprise stab at him. They wore war paint on their faces. It was no wonder they were still asleep. The camp had been up through the night, dancing to the war drums. It sent a bittersweet satisfaction through him, evidence that he had guessed right. Suddenly a half shout sounded, then another, and in seconds the camp was awake, and Fargo was surrounded by half-naked figures peering in astonishment at him. He didn't move as the voices grew louder, joined by squaws from the tipis. Only when the flap of the tipi nearest him opened and Strong Wing stepped out did Fargo unfold himself and rise to his feet.

The Cheyenne chief stared at him, unable to keep astonishment from his broad-cheeked face. "You must be a madman. What are you called?" the Indian questioned.

"I am called Fargo, and I am not a madman," he said. "I have come to stop the killing."

"What killing?" the chief asked, his voice flat.

"The Cheyenne and the soldiers," Fargo said.

"You come because you care about the Cheyenne?" the chief said, a sneer in his voice and the question.

"I care about my friends. I do not want them to die," Fargo said. The chief's grunt was an acceptance of his honesty. "The two men who came lied to Strong Wing," Fargo added and saw the surprise cross the heavy face.

"You know about this?" He frowned.

"I watched. I was very near," Fargo said.

"You are very brave or very foolish," the chief said, his eyes narrowing.

"Perhaps I am both," Fargo said and drew a deep breath. This was it, the moment he'd learn if he had guessed right about the major's plan. "The man told Strong Wing there would only be a handful of soldiers at the fort. He told Strong Wing it would be easy to kill everyone there," Fargo said.

The Indian waited and finally nodded. "That is what he said," he answered.

Fargo managed to stifle his cry of triumph. He had guessed right. He used his hands in sign language as he went on. "He set a trap for the Cheyenne," Fargo said. "There will be many more soldiers coming, enough to kill all the Cheyenne by surprise." The chief's black eyes seemed to pierce him as the man all but stared through him. "They will strike while you are attacking the fort. You will be taken by surprise. That is the trap he has set." Fargo paused and searched the chief's impassive face. "Go, see for yourself, find the main force of the bluecoats. Then you can leave, before you are caught in the trap. Your warriors will live. My friends will live." He fell silent, aware he had done all he could to shape the way things would unfold, and surprise stabbed at him when the chief made a sudden motion with one hand. Four braves seized him at once, and he made no effort to twist away.

"You will stay here," the chief said. "If your words are true, maybe you will live. If they are not, you will die."

"This is not right," Fargo protested. "I came here in honor."

"You came to save your people," the chief snapped, then reached out and pulled Fargo's gun from its holster. He tossed it into the tipi as the four braves led Fargo to a stake set into the ground at one edge of the camp. They tied his wrists together with a length of rawhide and then bound him to the stake with another strip. He submitted quietly as he saw that the rawhide was long enough to let him reach his legs. Watching in silence, he saw Strong Wing gather his braves and their ponies and, with a series of barked commands, he led the way out of the camp. As they rode off, they erupted in a raucous cacophony of high-pitched war cries that rang in his ears until they finally faded away in the woods.

He let his eyes sweep the camp. They had left only squaws, children, and two braves, who took up positions in front of a nearby tipi where they could survey the length of the camp. Fargo's mouth was a thin line as grimness swept through him. He had to free himself. The timetable had been set in motion, each event inexorably moving toward the final conclusion. It was vital he get the wagons to the fort to their place in the convergence of deceit, death, and truth. Lowering himself to the ground, he positioned his body against the stake and rested there as he stole both bound hands down to his calf. He inched his fingers downward, his eyes on the two guards. They only shot occasional glances at him as they talked to various squaws that came over to them. Overconfidence, he grunted, and was glad to see it. Slowly, ever so slowly, his fingers crept down along his leg and rested against the bottom of his trousers at his calf.

His eyes on the two guards, he waited till both were busy with a squaw and two children, quickly slid his hand up inside the trouser leg, and his fingers curled around the hilt of the thin blade and pulled it from the holster. He pulled his hand away from his leg and let the knife fall to the ground against his calf as one of the guards flicked a glance his way. When the man looked away, he pulled the thin, razor-sharp blade from inside his trouser leg and brought it up alongside his leg, letting his hand and the side of his trousers keep it covered. Drawing both legs up so that his knees were almost against his chest, he brought the knife into his lap, holding it with the fingers of both hands. His upraised knees shielded his lap and hands from sight, and the two guards continued tossing only occasional glances at him as he sat against the stake. Maneuvering the knife with his fingers, he turned the sharp point of the blade upward toward his chest.

Keeping his knees upraised, his hands in his lap shielded from the guards' view, he began to cut the rawhide. Able to make only short little motions with the knife, his fingers grew stiff quickly, and he had to pause to keep them from cramping up entirely. But the knife was razor sharp, and he felt even the little cuts digging into the bonds. When he saw one of the guards start to come closer to look at him, he slipped the blade through the front of his trousers and let it rest against his crotch. The guard paused before him, peered at him, then finally returned to the tipi. Raising his knees again, Fargo pulled the knife from inside his trousers and returned to his cramped cutting. He estimated that perhaps an hour had passed when he felt the rawhide around his wrists give way. He stayed in place, rested a few minutes, and then began to saw through the length of hide that bound him to the stake.

His wrists free, he had more opportunity to draw the blade in longer strokes, and, his knees still drawn up, he cut through the thong in half the time it had taken to do his wrist bonds. He shifted his body against the stake so that he almost faced the two guards at the tipi. Both had tomahawks in the waistbands of their breechclouts, and one carried a skinning knife in a leather pouch. Fargo knew there'd be no time for mercy. He'd have to take out both men at once, and he dropped the thin throwing knife into the palm of his hand. His eyes narrowed as he measured the distance to the two guards, closed his fingers around the hilt of the knife, and drew upon every ounce of strength in his wrist and arm muscles. The blade hurtled through the air in a slightly upward line, a faint whistling sound in its flight. One of the guards turned, caught sight of the thin shaft streaking at him, tried to dive away as his jaw fell open, and had time only to feel the blade slam through the side of his neck. He uttered a gargled sound as he fell sideways, hit the ground first on his knees as he yanked the blade from his throat, then fell facedown as a torrent of red cascaded from his neck.

Fargo was on his feet before the guard hit the ground, streaking bent over at the second guard. The Cheyenne yanked his tomahawk from the thong of his waistband and swung it in an upward arc. But he was too quick, his blow passing in front of Fargo's face. He tried to bring the tomahawk back, but Fargo plowed into him, crashing his left shoulder into the Indian's abdomen. The Cheyenne grunted as he fell backward and doubled over, the tomahawk out of position for another blow. Fargo's swinging left caught the man on the point of the jaw, and he staggered backward. Fargo's pile-driver right followed, landing at the same spot on the man's jaw. The Indian twisted almost entirely around as he fell, his crotch landing heavily on top of the edge of the tomahawk.

He cried out, a gasp of pain as he writhed on the ground. But Fargo was already racing to the other figure where he yanked the throwing knife free, paused to wipe it clean on the grass, and started toward the tipi. A glance at the squaws showed they were frozen in place with alarm and surprise, their eyes on him as he plunged into the tipi and scooped the Colt up from the ground. Dropping the knife into its calf holster, he held the Colt in his hand as he emerged from the tipi to find that the squaws were no longer frozen in place. Many had picked up stone-tipped lances from the camp, and others had stones, and a few had tomahawks. A half dozen spears hurtled through the air at him, and he ducked, twisted, and saw two of the lances hit the ground inches from his feet. He fired two shots into the ground at the feet of the onrushing squaws. It made them draw back and gave him the moment he wanted to race into the trees. When he reached the Ovaro, he untied the horse and climbed into the saddle. The calls and cries of the squaws faded away, and he sent the horse into a fast canter.

He rode hard, making no attempt to check on Strong Wing. The Cheyenne chief wouldn't be riding hard with his braves, Fargo knew. He'd be riding to draw near Fort Sanders where he could survey the situation, not to be there first. Fargo kept the Ovaro on as straight a path as he could to return to the steep draw beside the little lake, and he hoped the wagons were still in place. He'd been gone longer than he'd anticipated. The day drew to an end, then turned into night, and the moon hung low over the distant mountains when he reached the tree-covered, steep draw.

He rode down the strip of land, and a sigh of relief escaped him as he saw the clustered wagons near the lake. Most of the occupants were already asleep, but he saw Derek Hogath and Alison come toward him as he rode to a halt and dismounted. "Good God, you're here," Hogath said. "We were deciding to go on come morning. We figured something must have happened to you."

"Close enough," Fargo said and gratefully accepted the cup of coffee Hogath offered. In Alison's eyes he saw concern as well as questions.

"I don't see any troopers with you," she observed.

"The major has other plans," he grunted. "The major is behind everything that's happened."

"My God," Hogath said in shock. "I can't believe it."

"Believe it," Fargo said grimly and told them what he'd found out since he rode away, holding back only a few key pieces he still wanted to pursue on his own.

"Why? How does he fit into all this?" Alison asked.

"I've some thoughts on that, but I want to be sure of them, and that means confronting Foster again. Right now, the important thing is to get you to the fort," Fargo said.

"Where the major will be waiting," Hogath said. "What makes you think he'll let Alison meet with the official party?"

"He figured it might be impossible to prevent that so he made his own plans to see that whatever she tells the official party will never go any further."

"Because he's sent the Cheyenne to attack," Alison said.

"That's right. He arranged to have the official party and everyone at the fort killed, but he's also arranged a gigantic double-cross for the Cheyenne so they'll be wiped out, too," Fargo said. "Only it won't happen like that if it goes the way I set it up."

"If," Alison sniffed.

Fargo grimaced. "It's a big if, I'll admit, but it's the only one we've got. Remember, the major doesn't know that I know about his role. I want it kept that way for now. That means don't tell any of the others. I don't want them giving anything away by a wrong look, a word, an attitude."

"Understood," Hogath said. "What happened to that man Kosta?"

"There never was any Kosta," Fargo said, and Hogath frowned.

"But you were told the man who did all the hiring gave his name as Kosta," Hogath said.

Fargo allowed a wry smile to touch his lips for an instant. "So I was. I didn't put it together until I found out about the major. I was told the man spoke through a cloth mask that covered his face. It also distorted his speech. My man heard Kosta when it was Foster."

Hogath turned away shaking his head, the shock still in his face, and Alison followed to a wide-branched oak where Fargo unsaddled the horse. "Now, I'm going to get a night's sleep," he said.

Her hands rested against his chest. "I'm glad you're back. I was so afraid. How long till we reach the fort?" she asked.

"Another day. Morning after tomorrow, I'd guess," he said and felt her lips against his, soft, sweet touching, the warmth of her breasts pressing into his chest until she stepped back. "For coming back," she murmured.

"I knew I had a reason," he said, and she allowed a tiny smile as she hurried away. He undressed and lay down on his bedroll and knew as he went to sleep that the wheels he had set in motion were on a precarious axle with sudden death the real wagon master.

7

When morning came, Fargo led the wagons out of the draw and stayed close to long stands of red ash and cottonwoods. He found a pond to rest and water the horses in the heat of midday and paused beside Derek Hogath and Alison. "You keep moving straight north. Don't overheat your horses. I'm going to ride ahead," he said.

"I'd like to ride along," Alison put in.

"Get your horse," Fargo said and waited until she returned on the long-legged bay gelding. She rode off with him as the wagons began to roll, and he set a good pace as he explored through woodland, along ridges, letting his eyes sweep the terrain in all directions. He saw plenty of Indian pony prints, but they were all old. Strong Wing and his braves were off to the right somewhere, he guessed, probably at least a few hours back. They lost still more time as they carefully searched for signs of Lieutenant Bowdon and his full garrison, and that was exactly how Fargo had expected it would go. The distant shapes of the Black Hills appeared to his left as Fargo halted atop a ridge where a big sumac afforded shade over a circle of soft broom moss. The day had grown hot, and Fargo dismounted and put the Ovaro in the shade of the sumac. Alison did the same and returned to where he was stretched out on the moss.

"I want the horses fresh when we need them," he said as she sank down beside him.

"How far behind us are the wagons?" Alison asked.

"An hour, maybe a little more," he said.

"When we reach Fort Sanders tomorrow, it could all go wrong, couldn't it?" she questioned.

"I'm banking it won't," he said and knew he was leaning more on hope than certainty.

"But it could," she pressed.

"It could," he admitted.

"I want something for myself if that should happen. I don't want to risk coming away with nothing," she said.

"What'd you have in mind?" he asked. Her eyes stayed on his as her arms lifted and encircled his neck.

"I told myself if you came back safe I wouldn't wait and hope for another chance. I'm not strong enough for that," she said, and her lips pressed his, a harsh kiss, then softening to linger as her fingers pulled open buttons. She shrugged her shoulders, and her shirt fell away, and his eyes moved across the lovely breasts, full and very round, creamy-smooth skin, each cup very rounded, each tipped with an almost flat little nipple of the palest pink set on a small, equally pale pink areola. She slid her skirt off and let him take in all of her with an almost defiant gleam in her eyes. The warm yellow sunlight bathed her in a soft glow, and his eyes lingered on her softly convex little belly, its roundness its own kind of sensuousness, and below it, a full, dark triangle with a very round, almost fat little Venus mound.

Below the provocative triangle, smooth, full thighs were beautifully shaped with nice round knees, no edges to her, even her elbows rounded, nothing that jarred the way every part of her flowed into every other. She had a rounded seamlessness that gave her a strange combination of simmering sensualness and happy cuddliness. But as he shed clothes, her hands came to him and moved across the smooth, muscled contours of his chest, explored downward, and her sudden gasp was all sensual. Her mouth came to his, open, drawing his lips, his tongue, working, answering with her own tongue and small gasped groans. He brought her onto the soft broom moss, caressed the very round breasts, and she cried out as she brought her knees up, legs held tightly together. His mouth moved downward, kissed the creamy skin, found the flat, pale pink nipple of one breast, and gently pulled on it.

"Oh, oh . . . oh, yes," Alison murmured and pushed her breast upward. "More, take more," she cried softly, and he pulled again on the very round mound. He let his tongue move back and forth over the very flat tip and felt it grow, not very much, but enough to take on a tiny firmness of its own. Her hand reached up, closed around the bottom of her breast, and pushed the soft mound deeper into his mouth as she gave a long groan. He caressed her breast again, pulled gently, then not so gently, and she cried out in pleasure. Finally, his lips slid from the soft, creamy mound, moved down across her abdomen, nibbled around the round little indentation, and his hand found the dark triangle. He pressed into the soft Venus mound, deliciously soft, ran his fingers through the soft-wire nap, and touched the tip of the inverted *V*. "Yes, oh, God, yes . . . oh, God," Alison gasped, and her knees rose up, legs still held tightly together as she swung them from side to side.

He let his hand stay and pressed gently into the insides of her thighs as she continued to keep her legs together. He pushed a little deeper and felt the dampness of her skin, moved his hand again, and Alison moaned, a long, wavering sound, and suddenly her legs came open, slammed together again, and fell open at once. He ran his palm into the triangle again, against the very soft little mound, pressed, then slid down to the tip of the triangle once more. This time Alison only gasped as her thighs stayed apart, and he gently touched and heard her scream. "Don't stop . . . Jesus, don't stop," she demanded, and her hips rose, lifted higher, and he touched the edge of the sequacious lips, touched their wet softness as Alison's cries rose, grew higher and louder, and he heard the voice of Eros, the cry of Circe. His pulsating firmness came against her, touched her inner thighs, and Alison screamed, and her hand flew down, finding him, clutching itself around him as she gave tiny spasms that shook her entire body.

Her hand stayed around him, the pleasure of sensual possessiveness in her grip. "Oh, yes, yes . . . oh, yes," Alison breathed and pulled at him, brought him up to the dark portal, and now she was pulling harder, turning her hips to welcome his firm hotness. There was no holding back for her. She was entirely captured by her own hungers, runaway wanting, almost a desperation to her as she gasped tiny sounds. He moved forward and let his throbbing head touch her, resting at the very edge of the velvet lips. "Jesus, oh, oh, oh . . . oh, my God, my God," Alison almost screamed and thrust herself upward. He slid deeper, rubbing against the sweet cusp, and in Alison's cries he heard the wonder and awe of her body wakening in ways it had never wakened before. Her full, smooth thighs rose up to come against him, rubbing up and down along his sides as her pelvis thrust upward in long, heaving motions. "More, aaaagh . . . more," Alison cried, her voice dropping low, becoming a gargled moan, and he moved back and forth inside the moist glove.

As he moved in her, with her, for her, increasing the wonderful rhythm of ecstasy, Alison's legs rose to clasp around him, and she pulled his face down to her breasts. The sun bathed them in its heat, and he felt the sweet wetness of her body against his as they commingled fluids, inner and outer. He heard his own groans of pleasure rising with hers when suddenly her fingers dug into his back, curled against him. "Now," she gasped. "Oh, God, now," she screamed, her voice rising. "Now, now, now, now," and her entire body shook, round breasts leaping upward, falling from one side to the other. He felt himself being carried along with her explosion of pure passion, and her contractions flowed around him, unseen embraces of ecstasy.

When Alison's voice rose in a muffled scream, her mouth pressed into his chest, it was that singular cry of too much and too little, rapture and protest, eternal victory and eternal defeat. She quivered for a long moment before she fell back onto the moss and lay on her back, her eyes looking up at him with the awe and wonder still in their dark blue depths. His own gaze stayed on her smooth-skinned, seamless loveliness and enjoyed the complete relaxation of her that wrapped her in an added indolent beauty. He drew an invisible line over her nakedness with one hand, touching, pausing, tracing, as though he could use touch to imprint her in his mind. She reached arms up, encircled his neck, and pulled his face down to her breasts where he stayed and enjoyed the sweet smothering. But, finally, he rose to his feet and pulled her up with him. "We'll be having company soon," he said, and she returned a rueful nod as she reached for her clothes.

They had just finished dressing when he caught the sudden movement in the trees only a dozen yards away. He pulled Alison deeper under the sumac where the horses grazed. "Not the company I had in mind," Fargo whispered and watched the lone rider come out of the trees, moving slowly on his pony as he scanned the terrain, the Cheyenne markings on his armband. He watched the Indian go by and disappear into the cottonwoods beyond before he gathered Alison's horse and the Ovaro. Alison peered at him with that sharp way of hers. "You're not that upset," she said.

"No. He's an outrider scouting. I expected as much," Fargo said. "It means Strong Wing's following somewhere east of us."

"You think he saw the wagons?" Alison asked.

"I'd guess so, and that's good. It'll confirm the things I told him. Besides, he's not interested in the wagons, not yet," Fargo said and turned as he caught the squeak of a wheel. Alison followed him as he swung onto the pinto and rode from under the big sumac to meet the wagons that rolled into view. He led the way north over a long strip of flat land, and when night descended, the stark shapes of the Black Hills were clearly outlined. "Two hours riding come morning ought to bring us to Fort Sanders," he told Hogath when the supper meal ended. He departed from his usual practice and lay down near the wagons where he received a brief visit from Alison as she went to get water from a small stream. She fastened a glance of sardonic amusement on him.

125

"Afraid or exhausted?" she remarked.

The softness of his voice didn't cloak anything entirely, but just covered an icy edge. "Not the first and don't want to be the second. Tomorrow's going to take everything I've got and everything you've got. Go to sleep," he said. She swallowed hard, turned, and hurried away, acceptance without concession. But that was like her, he thought smiling as he drew sleep around himself.

When morning came, he rode a few thousand yards ahead of the wagons, but kept them in sight as he crossed back and forth in the shadow of the Black Hills. He sought a glimpse of uniforms, found none, but refused to be bothered. If the lieutenant was on schedule, he'd still be a few hours away, and Fargo waved the wagons onto the wide, flat plains that stretched ahead, and he could feel the excitement that rose up from the wagons as he rode back alongside them for a while. Except for Alison and Brenda, Pearl, and Ida Bluebell. In their faces he saw only anxiety.

The miles rolled away; the sun moved toward the noon hour sky, and he led the wagons along the plain bordered by two large forests of red ash. They had just moved to the end of the trees when he saw the fort rising up from the sagebrush that dotted the plain. He took in a sturdy stockade with block houses built into the two front corners of the structure, and he was still scanning the new fort when three riders moved in between him and the stockade. He saw Major Foster at once, two of his troopers with him, and the major came to a halt as Fargo moved closer with the wagons. He saw the tension in the major's face as he peered past the oncoming wagons to the forests of red ash directly behind them. A grim smile tried to form on Fargo's lips, but he kept his face impassive. His quick glance at the new fort saw the flagpole was still without a flag. The dedication hadn't been rushed through overnight, he was happy to see. With a wave of his hand he slowed the wagons as he came up to the major and the two troopers.

"Seems you all made it through," the major said, and Fargo saw his eyes flick to the distant trees. In fact, the major had difficulty in returning his eyes to Fargo and the wagons. "Have them form a line twenty yards from the fort," Foster said coldly.

"That'll do for now. They'll be taking a few days to choose their land and stake out claims," Fargo said and saw the major's eyes were scanning the trees again. "You looking for somebody?" Fargo asked mildly.

"Just being alert," Foster snapped.

Fargo rode closer to the new fort as the wagons followed, and he took in the fort with care and admiration. The stockade poles were tall, broad, and well caulked, the front gate wide but easy to close. However, it was the blockhouses that held his attention. The logs of each were cut flat on both upper and lower sides and carefully notched to lie tight against each other and permit no cracks between them. That made for flat walls almost impossible for attackers to get a foothold for climbing. Each had a stone chimney and plenty of rifle holes cut into the walls for defenders to fire back at their attackers, each planned so that relatively few men could defend a wide area of the fort. It had obviously been planned to act as a bastion against attacks by any combination of the powerful Northern Plains tribes as well as excursions by the Central Plains and the north of the border tribes.

As the wagons rolled closer, he had them halt in a line outside the stockade walls, Alison's wagons almost in front of the gate. Fargo dismounted as he saw the major swing from his horse and bark orders to three more troopers. "Take up guard positions. Keep your eyes on the trees," Foster ordered as his eyes still swept the distant tree line. Fargo halted beside Alison, cautious satisfaction in his voice.

"They listened to me. They're hanging back, and Foster's sweating bullets," he muttered. "Get Brenda and the others and all your documents. The moment you wanted is here." Alison swung herself around and disappeared inside her wagon, and Fargo moved toward the major. "I'll be taking those young ladies I told you about in to see the official party," he said and saw Foster's face tighten.

"That'll have to wait till after the dedication," the major said as he faced Fargo, drawing himself up in his best bantam-rooster manner. But his eyes again flicked to the trees. He was desperately buying time, making a last stop-gap effort as he wondered what was holding back everything he'd set up. But Foster had to be stopped, Fargo realized. There were too many imponderables hanging fire, too many things that could go wrong for everyone. Alison had to get to the officials, and Fargo turned to the major.

"Why?" Fargo asked.

"The official party is here to dedicate this fort. That's their first order of business, not to take up time with a list of wild accusations. You'll have to hold off on that," Foster said.

"They've come too far at too big a price for holding off," Fargo said.

The major gave him a frowning stare. "Are you daring to contradict me, mister? I can make you the first tenant in the fort's guardhouse. All I have to do is give an order."

Fargo gave a deep sigh as Alison came toward him, Brenda, Pearl, and Ida Bluebell with her. Alison and Brenda carried small leather pouches. Fargo offered the major a smile. "Take us to the officials," he said.

"I see I'm going to have to give that order," Foster bit out.

Fargo's smile stayed as his hand rested on the butt of the Colt. "That would be a major mistake," he said, "if you don't mind the pun. You make one wrong move, and you'll have a bullet between your eyes before you can blink. Count on it."

Foster stared at him. "You'd be shot down at once," he said.

"Maybe, but you'll be too dead to see it," Fargo said.

"You're a madman, Fargo," the major said.

"Yes, sir, more or less," Fargo said almost pleasantly, but his lake blue eyes were cold as ice floes. Fargo silently enjoyed the tiny beads of perspiration that suddenly covered the major's face. It was plain he realized he was facing no idle threat. "Now, these ladies are going to meet with the official party. I'll be watching you every minute, every damn minute, so you'd best be real careful. Let's go," Fargo said and started forward close beside the major. As they entered the fort, he saw Foster turn to cast another glance back at the trees. When he moved on, his jaw muscles were twitching. "You look real nervous. Something else bothering you, Major?" Fargo asked blandly.

"Just you and this obsession to disrupt the dedication of a United States fort," Foster rasped. Fargo smiled inwardly and saw the rest of the major's handful of troops were in the fort near the gate. "Stay alert," Foster snapped at them. "Yell if you see anything."

He strode on, and Fargo stayed at his side and took in the buildings inside the fort, officers' quarters and the long barracks building at the rear near the stable. Five men were gathered outside what was going to be the company mess hall but was still largely empty except for a long table. One figure, tall, silver-haired with a patrician nose and a commanding presence, wearing a dark blue frock coat, turned to the major as they approached. "We're ready, Major, but frankly we're a little disappointed. We expected a full turnout of the garrison for the occasion, plus we understood there'd be new settlers," he said.

"The new settlers are here," Fargo answered. "I just brought them."

"And you are?" the man queried.

"Skye Fargo. Some folks call me the Trailsman," Fargo said.

"Senator Connolly. I represent the President of the United States," the man said, and Fargo's eyes went to a trim figure wearing the uniform of an army general.

"General Hawkins, army chief of staff," the man introduced.

"Senator Williams," another man said. "Military Affairs Committee, and this is my colleague, Senator Drew."

A tall, thin figure in a formal striped suit spoke up. "Herbert Matso, secretary of the army," he said and turned a thin, lined face to Alison. "I trust there are more settlers than you four young ladies," he said.

"The others are outside," Fargo said and glanced at Foster who, he could see, was inwardly seething. "But these are four very special young ladies. I think you ought to listen to what they have to say before you go on with the dedication."

Senator Connolly's brows lifted. "Indeed?" he said.

"They have things you'll want to hear, and a lot of people have been killed to stop them from getting here," Fargo answered.

The senator frowned at his words. "People killed?" he echoed.

"Please hear us out, gentlemen," Alison said.

"This is most unusual," General Hawkins said.

"It is. That's why we're here," Alison said.

"Perhaps we should go inside," the senator said and started to enter the mess hall. The others followed, and Fargo entered last, closing the door behind him as he stood near the major. Connolly cast a glance at him. "You always keep one hand on your gun, Mister Fargo?" he asked.

"Bad habit." Fargo smiled and took his hand from the butt of the Colt. There was nothing Foster could do now to stop Alison from speaking her piece. He'd have to stand and listen as he sweated away the minutes, wondering why the Cheyenne still hadn't attacked. Fargo positioned himself a few feet from the major as Senator Connolly and the other dignitaries lined up on one side of the long table. Alison faced them with Brenda, Pearl, and Ida flanking her.

"We're listening," the senator said, and Alison opened her leather pouch and spread its contents on the table.

"I'm Alison Carter. My father was Captain Alistair Carter, United States Cavalry," Alison began quietly, but instantly came out swinging, trampling over diplomacy, protocol, tradition, and suspicion. She struck with bold words infused with bitter anger too vivid to question.

"There was a man who lied, cheated, and murdered to get what he wanted, the rank of general in the United States Army. This was a man who dishonored his uniform, his service, and his country. We're here to stop you from honoring this man because he deserves no honor. We're here to stop you from making a mockery of everything the United States Army stands for by honoring Billy Sanders, the man who valued only one thing in life, his own ambition."

Her angry denunciation cast its spell, Fargo saw, her listeners riveted in place. She quickly began to present the details she had outlined for him, starting with the massacre of the Ponca women and children, the general's false claims and fake burials. She left out nothing and presented the letter her father had written, followed with the treachery of sending her father's patrol out to be slaughtered. She introduced Brenda next, and let Brenda tell about her younger brother and all that had happened to him.

Pearl followed and told how her fiancé had known Sanders lied about the Ponca warriors fleeing south so he could set it up for the Indians to annihilate the troop led by the one man who planned to speak out against him, Alison's father. Alison saved Ida Bluebell for last, and Ida told of the massacre of the Ponca children and women, which the general had led. She spoke quietly, with all the detail and heart-wrenching anguish of one who had witnessed it and lived never to forget. When she finished, Fargo's eyes swept Senator Connolly and the others and saw shock, revulsion, and anger, and in the face of General Hawkins, a terrible shame. It was Connolly who found his voice first.

"This is a shocking and terrible story you brought to

us," he said. "You understand it will take us some time to go over it again and evaluate it. We'll submit all of it to the Military Affairs Committee, and I assure you we'll investigate every bit of it. We'll even have that burial site dug up."

"That will prove everything we've told you," Alison said.

"We must investigate, you understand, but I think I can speak for all of us when I tell you that I am satisfied you've told us the truth of this sorry and terrible affair," Connolly said.

"I'd say we owe you all a debt of gratitude," Herbert Matso cut in. "As secretary of the army, I am grateful for your having saved us from perpetuating a terrible wrong and soiling the name of the United States Army.

Fargo's eyes went to the major and saw icy rage held back in the man's face. But he also saw confusion, Foster's head inclined slightly to one side as he still listened for the Cheyenne. "They're not coming," Fargo said quietly, and Foster stared at him, still unable to understand what had gone wrong.

Senator Connolly's voice cut in as he spoke to Alison. "Of course, there will be no dedication of this fort now," he said. "But we are going to approve keeping this new facility manned and in operation. The need for its existence remains. In time, we will decide on a proper name for it." Alison nodded and moved to one side and found the major only a few feet from her. Fargo saw the senator turn to him. "Mister Fargo, you said a lot of people were killed to stop these young ladies from reaching us. That says there are those who wanted to prevent the truth from coming out."

"That's right," Fargo grunted.

"You have any idea who?" Connolly asked.

"I know exactly who," Fargo said as his eyes went to Foster. "That lying little weasel," he said and saw the rage in Foster's face.

"That's ridiculous," Foster snapped. "This man is given to making wild accusations. It's known all over. He's lying just to make himself important."

The senator's eyes held on Fargo. "You have any proof of such a serious charge?" he asked.

Fargo answered, but his eyes were on the major. "Ask him why he brought you here with only a handful of troops," Fargo said.

"The rest of my men are on the way. The senator knows that. They're just a little late," Foster said.

"Because you planned for them to be late, only they should have been here by now," Fargo said, his eyes still boring into the major. "You made a deal with the Cheyenne. You told them there'd be only a handful of troops here and they could kill everybody," he flung out and saw Foster's tongue flick over his lips. Fargo turned to Connolly and the others. "There's only one reason that hasn't happened. There's only one reason you're not all dead the way he planned it. I got to the Cheyenne. I made a change in his plans."

"I tell you this is preposterous. The man's a lunatic," Foster shouted. "Why would I want to protect General Sanders's name? What reason would I have?"

"This reason," Fargo snapped, reached into his pocket, and threw the daguerreotype on the table and enjoyed the astonishment that flooded the major's face.

"Where'd you get that?" Foster asked, his voice cracking.

"Out of the bottom of your trunk," Fargo threw back

and turned again to Senator Connolly. "That's a picture of him when he was about eight years old, I'd guess." Fargo turned the daguerreotype over to show the back. "Those initials there are E.S., and they stand for Elmont Sanders. He's General Sanders's bastard son."

"The woman in Washington," Alison's voice gasped.

"Probably," Fargo said. "I also found extra blank birth certificates that let the general turn Elmont Sanders into Elmont Foster, complete with a new birthday and new identity to go with his new name. Then, over the years, he signed all the proper papers that got young Elmont Foster into the Military Academy. He also recommended him for every promotion after he graduated, no doubt over more deserving young officers. Of course, the relationship was a closely guarded secret, but it was one more part of General Sanders, maybe not so different from his massacre of women and children to win himself a general's stars."

"My God," the senator breathed.

"That's why the major had to try and stop the truth about General Sanders from coming out. It would have shown him to be a man who had lived a lie all his life, a man who had cheated, deceived, forged, and murdered to protect himself and his ambition. And his son is no damn better," Fargo finished.

"You bastard," the major's voice screamed, and as Fargo saw the flash of movement, he yanked at his Colt, but Foster was at Alison's side, his army Remington held to her temple. "Don't anybody move or she gets it," he threatened, holding his other arm around Alison's waist. "Take the bullets out of your gun, Fargo," he ordered. "Carefully." Fargo searched Foster's eyes and saw a desperate man, one who could be pushed into squeezing the trigger by the slightest thing. Fargo flipped the chamber of the Colt and let the bullets fall to the floor. "Throw the gun away," Foster rasped, and Fargo sent the Colt skittering across the mess hall floor. Keeping the pistol at Alison's temple, Foster started toward the door, pausing as he neared it. "Anyone comes after me, she's dead," he said, backed from the building, and pushed the door shut.

Fargo saw the others turn to him, Brenda starting to go to the door. "Don't. He means it," Fargo said, and she halted.

"We can't just wait here," Brenda protested.

"No, but we can't crowd him. He's on the edge. It'd be curtains for Alison," Fargo said and stepped to the door, then stayed for a little more than a minute with his hand on the doorknob before he pulled the door open. He stepped outside, Brenda at his heels, the others crowding after her, and he stopped in his tracks. A line of troopers, their carbines raised, faced the doorway.

"Get back," a corporal ordered.

"Easy, soldier. There are things you don't know," Fargo said.

"Stay inside. The major's orders," the corporal returned.

"Listen to me, soldier. Put the rifles down," Fargo tried again.

"Inside. Major's orders," the trooper said adamantly, his voice hardening. Fargo felt the figure brush past him and saw General Hawkins push forward.

"Goddammit, Corporal, put those carbines down. You see the stars on this uniform?" he barked.

"Yes, sir," the trooper said. "But—"

"I gave you an order, trooper," the general roared. "I

hope you know that an order from a general overrides one from a major."

"Yes, sir," the corporal said and lowered his carbine along with the rest of the troopers. Fargo dashed past them to the Ovaro, vaulted onto the horse, and raced from the fort. Outside the gate Derek Hogath gestured frantically from atop his wagon, and Fargo sent the Ovaro south at a full gallop. He strained his ears when he reached the red ash as he tried to pick up the sound of the major's horse over the hoofbeats of the Ovaro. It took another minute, but he finally picked up the sound of the other horse and slowed at once, then speeded up again as he veered to his right. He drew the big Henry from its saddle case as he rode and finally glimpsed the major fleeing through the trees, Alison held in front of him in the saddle.

Fargo raised the rifle and just as quickly lowered it. Foster was twisting and turning his mount and had Alison too close against him to allow a clear shot. The Ovaro had almost drawn abreast of the major when the major's head swiveled and Fargo cursed. Foster had heard him, and Fargo saw the man raise his pistol and put it to Alison's head. Halting behind a thick red ash, Foster called out, "That's got to be you, Fargo. Keep after me and I'll kill her."

Fargo stayed silent, but knew Foster had made no idle threat. He kept the Ovaro still, and Foster raced his mount away, still holding the gun to Alison. Fargo spit out curses. To pursue would mean Alison's death. But Foster was sure to kill and discard her when he got far enough away. Alison's fate seemed not so much a matter of what but simply when. Fargo weighed his two wretched options and decided he could not let Foster decide the outcome. He spurred the pinto forward, closed distance again, but stayed back, able to catch only glimpses of the major as he fled. Foster had lowered the pistol from Alison's temple to concentrate on getting more speed out of his horse, but he still offered no target, Fargo swore. Fargo felt his mouth draw tight in a thin line as he again weighed the risks of drawing closer to find a moment to shoot. He was watching the major's mount skirt around a trunk of a thick, old tree when, with silent, deadly suddenness, a sheaf of arrows winged through the air. Two missed altogether, two struck Foster high on the shoulder blade, and a third ripped through his arm. Fargo saw him pitch from the horse and take Alison with him. He also saw an arrow graze her head.

Fargo yanked the pinto to a halt and leaped to the ground behind a tree as Foster fired back from one knee at the half-naked figures that darted from the foliage. He fired over Alison, who lay facedown, and Fargo saw another hail of arrows swish silently at the two figures on the ground. Two arrows bracketed Alison within inches of her head, and another arrow plunged into the major's arm. The pistol fell from his hand as he gasped in pain, and tried to twist away, but another arrow buried itself into his thigh. He cried out again as he fell on his side, and Fargo saw Alison roll away, and almost hit against two Cheyenne warriors who came through the trees. They grabbed her and yanked her to her feet. Fargo stayed low and saw Strong Wing stride up to where a half dozen braves had Foster surrounded.

"You set trap for Cheyenne, snake-tongued devil," the Cheyenne chief said, and Fargo grunted silently. It wasn't hard to put it all together. The Cheyenne had seen the lieutenant's full complement of troopers riding hard to the fort, stayed low, and let them go on, unwilling to mount an attack on an entire cavalry brigade. But they had stayed in the forest and waited, perhaps just to see what else unexpected might occur. What they finally saw was the major racing away with Alison. Foster glared at Strong Wing, unable to understand what the chief had said to him, but aware he had to make some reply.

"Where the hell were you? Why didn't you attack the fort?" he spit out. With no interpreter there, the chief didn't understand Foster, but he understood the only important thing to him. "You set trap for Cheyenne," he repeated, raised his arm, and the half dozen braves who surrounded Foster drew their short bows back and fired directly into the major. They fired a second volley and then a third, and Fargo saw Alison turn away. When they finished, the major resembled a pincushion more than a human being. The Cheyenne chief administered the coup de grâce, an arrow into Foster's face, a gesture of contempt and revenge.

He motioned to the braves, and they held Alison as they led her away with them. Fargo swore under his breath. It was hardly the best moment, but he knew there would be no best moment. This one was as good as he could hope for. He rose, the rifle in his hand, and stepped from behind the tree. Strong Wing spun at once, his face hardening.

8

In the chief's eyes came surprise at first, then icy aware-
ness that there was but one way Fargo could have escaped the camp. "What do you want here?" he asked.

"I come for the woman," Fargo said as a dozen braves
gathered beside him. Others continued on with Alison.

"No," the chief said.

"She was not his woman," Fargo said.

"She ran with him. She is ours now," the Cheyenne
growled.

"I want her," Fargo said.

"No."

"This is not right. My words saved you," Fargo said.

"That is why you stand there alive," the Cheyenne
said. "Go. You will not get another chance."

Fargo's eyes flicked to the braves beside the chief. All
had arrows on their bowstrings. If he fired the Henry, it
would be his last shot, he knew and he slowly turned and
walked away. He didn't look back, but he heard the
Cheyenne move on through the trees, heard them mount
their ponies, and ride off. He halted beside the Ovaro
and rested on one knee. He knew they were returning to
camp. He'd wait. It would be his only chance. He rose,
took the horse to an area of grammagrass where it could

graze, and waited till dusk began to sift over the land. He continued to wait, let dusk become night, and only when the moon crossed the midnight sky did he swing into the saddle. He rode slowly through the darkness of the forest and reached the Cheyenne camp when the moon was only an hour from dawn and curving down the last of the night sky.

He dismounted when he saw the camp, tethered the Ovaro to a low branch, and crept forward. The camp lay before him, dark and silent, a low fire of embers casting a flickering light against the tipis. He scanned the length of the camp before he found Alison, tied hand and foot alongside the last of the tipis, kept in place by a length of rawhide that bound her to a heavy log. She lay on her side, and he swept the camp again, but there were no figures asleep on the ground, and he was thankful they had all decided to sleep inside the tipis. He crept forward on silent footsteps, darted across the open space near the fire, and reached Alison and covered her mouth with his hand. Her eyes snapped open and stared up at him. He paused a moment and slowly withdrew his hand as the first tint of pink touched the sky.

Alison's eyes held something he couldn't decipher as he drew the throwing knife from the calf holster to cut the length of rawhide that bound her to the log, but he saw her lips moving silently. They formed the word *go*, and she moved her head from side to side. He paused and frowned at her. She formed the word again with her lips. He was staring at her, trying to understand, when the flap of the tipi flew open. Strong Wing and four braves burst out, arrows drawn on their bows, each aimed at him. The Cheyenne chief stepped closer and lowered his bow as his braves surrounded Fargo. "I knew you would come," he grunted with contempt. "A woman can make a man twice a fool."

Fargo let a bitter sound fall from his lips. He knew now why there were no braves sleeping in the open, and he swore at himself. He had ignored his own first commandment, thou shalt not be careless. And he had failed to respect the cleverness of the Cheyenne. Another dozen braves stepped from nearby tipis, followed by others, as the chief pulled the Colt from Fargo's holster. Fargo rose and let the knife drop to the ground. At a motion from the chief, Alison was lifted to her feet. "Now you can watch my braves enjoy her, and then she can watch you die," the Cheyenne said as daylight began to flood the camp. A line of squaws emerged from the tipis and began to pull Alison's shirt off, then her skirt.

She refused to cringe, Fargo saw, and felt admiration and bitter helplessness. Sound vibrated in his ears suddenly, before it reached the Cheyenne, the pounding of hooves, and then he felt the sound through the soles of his feet. A silent shout of hope rose inside him as he stayed motionless.

The Cheyenne heard it but seconds later, and Fargo saw them turn, frowns sliding across their faces almost as one. The sound became more than hoofbeats, and Fargo heard the cracking of small low branches as horses raced through the forest, then the flat slap of bridle chains and the sudden barked command. Strong Wing's voice rose over everything as he shouted orders to his men. He turned and started to run past when Fargo dived and caught the Cheyenne chief at the knees. Strong Wing went down, and Fargo reached out, grabbed the Colt from the Indian's hand and pulled it free. He tried to turn his head, but the Cheyenne's kick caught him on the side of his face, and he cursed in pain as he fell back. The chief had regained his feet, and he was running past the tipi, Fargo saw, as were the other braves. Lying on his stomach, Fargo saw the Cheyenne disappear into the trees at the edge of the camp, and then his head swiveled as the line of troopers crashed into the camp from the other end, the lieutenant at the head of the column.

A hail of arrows met them from the trees, and Bowdon almost took two as he ducked low in the saddle. "Fall off," he yelled at his men, and the troopers peeled away to race out of the camp. Fargo glimpsed them halting, then dismounting to fire a volley across the camp into the trees, follow with another and still another. Fargo saw Alison sitting half up, unable to move, still held by the rawhide length to the log. Bullets were hitting the ground uncomfortably close and hurtling over her head as Fargo, staying on his stomach, crawled to her and began to cut the length of rawhide. Three bullets grazed Alison's head as the troopers exchanged bullets and arrows with the Cheyenne. When the knife cut through the rawhide, he pulled her down beside him as he dug at the thong binding her ankles.

It was quicker to part, but he held her down as he lifted his head and peered over her back. Just as he did, he saw Bowdon lead another charge across the camp, this time with half his men as the others stayed back and laid down a covering fire. But the Cheyenne filled the air with arrows that became a wall of death as they descended in a low arc, and Bowdon again ordered his men to fall off. Fargo seized the moment to pull the Alison with him as he rolled across the ground to come to a halt at the far side of the tipi. She crawled with him as he motioned for her to follow him, and he stayed on his stomach as he reached the trees. He put his finger to his lips, and Alison stayed silent as he listened. He caught the soft sound of moccasins moving through the forest to the left and to the right. Taking her hand in his, he rose to one knee and darted across a space between the tipi and the next one.

He dropped down behind the next tipi, measured the distance to the next nearest one, and darted forward again with Alison. The carbine fire erupted on both sides of them, and Fargo shouted in gratitude. Bowdon had seen them and was putting down a covering fire. Fargo took advantage of the protective shield to run to the other side of the camp and into the trees where the troopers had dug in. Alison clung to him, fingers digging into his arms as he rose and finally pulled her loose.

"God," she breathed.

"Got your voice back," he said, and she nodded; then he saw the lieutenant come toward him in a crouch.

"I'm real glad to see you," Fargo said.

"One good turn deserves another," Bowdon said.

"How'd you find us?" Fargo asked.

"We reached the fort soon after the major ran with Alison. General Hawkins gave me a quick briefing and sent us after you. We found the major's body and then picked up the Cheyenne's trail. We had to stop when it got dark, but I started off again before dawn. I took a guess they'd keep on through the forest. I guessed right," Bowdon said. "Now, we have the two of you, and that's what we came for, but I'm going to have another go at the bastards. I'd like to wipe them out."

"No," Fargo said.

"No?" The lieutenant frowned.

"You'll wipe yourself out," Fargo said. "They've already spread out in small pockets to return fire from different directions. Then they'll split up into smaller groups, run and fire, fire and run. This is their land, perfect for the kind of fighting they'll do. They have all the advantages. All you'll do is lose men and chase shadows."

"You're saying break off further pursuit," Bowdon grunted.

"Those are army words. I'm saying get the hell out of here before you lose a lot of good men," Fargo said.

"I'll be taking your advice on this," the lieutenant said.

"Don't keep your men grouped together where they'll make a concentrated target. Move out fast in single file and fire back on the run. They won't follow very far," Fargo said. The lieutenant hurried back to his men, barked tense commands, and Fargo went to the Ovaro with Alison. He swung her into the saddle behind him and gave her the Colt as he took the big Henry. He heard the lieutenant's shout and the sound of the troopers riding off at a fast canter. Their forms flashed into sight through the trees as Fargo spurred the Ovaro on to the left of the fleeing line of soldiers. The shouts of the Cheyenne rose as they gave chase, suddenly aware that their foe was making a getaway.

He saw arrows arc through the air from a dozen different directions, pass mostly to one side of where he and Alison rode, and he veered farther to the left. He charged through a thicket of five-foot-high burdock when the trees behind it moved, branches pushed back, and the Cheyenne chief and three of his braves came into view. The three braves had their bows raised, arrows in place, bowstrings drawn. But Fargo had the big Henry raised and aimed at the chief. Strong Wing's voice was a deep rumble.

"You shoot and you die. Woman, too," he said.

"I shoot and you die. First. Bullet faster than arrow," Fargo countered and refused to flinch. The moment had come, he knew, and saw the chief's eyes go to the rifle, then flick back to him. The Indian wasn't afraid to die, Fargo knew. That was not part of a Cheyenne chief. But Fargo fervently banked on something more. The chief was leader of his tribe. They depended on his leadership, gave their allegiance to him. They expected wisdom, not just fearlessness, and he knew his role was not simply bravery. Fargo knew the Cheyenne mentality well enough to put his own trust in that as the seconds seemed to go by as though they were hours.

But finally he saw the chief's shoulders drop, an almost imperceptible gesture, yet it told Fargo he had guessed right. "Another time will come," the chief said.

"It will," Fargo agreed as he lowered the rifle.

"I will remember you, big man. You are very brave and very wise, or a fool on whom the gods have smiled," the Cheyenne said, slowly turned his horse, and faded into the trees, his warriors following him.

Fargo sent the pinto forward. "They could just turn and kill us," Alison whispered.

"They won't. Their sense of honor would forbid that," Fargo said and put the pinto into a canter. The troopers were out of earshot, and only when he rode out of the woods did he glimpse the distant line of blue, now riding in a column of twos. The lieutenant slowed when he caught sight of Fargo and Alison, let them catch up, and brought his mount alongside them.

"I'm still having trouble believing what they told me about the major," he said, his young face serious.

"That's good. Never stop having trouble with it," Fargo said and drew a questioning glance from Bowdon. "It'll mean you'll never be disillusioned enough to understand a man such as the major. Or Sanders."

"Bad seed, bad fruit," Bowdon said. Fargo nodded and felt the grimness stab at him, and he rode in silence with Alison until the fort finally rose up before them. Derek Hogath and all the others were inside the fort along with Senator Connolly and the other dignitaries, and a cheer went up as Fargo and Alison rode in with the lieutenant. It was later, when dusk had descended and they'd all had a chance to wash and freshen up, that Fargo found Senator Connolly, General Hawkins, the lieutenant, and Alison, Pearl, Brenda, and Ida Bluebell in a little knot.

"Just in time to hear what we've officially decided," the senator said. "The lieutenant will be acting commander of the fort until we've finished our formal inquiry. And, in our official capacity, we've decided to give a name to this fort in honor of what these four young women have done. It will be called Fort Justice."

"I'd say that's a right proper name," Fargo said.

"Most of the garrison will stay here, but the lieutenant will send a detail to take us back come morning. I asked the young ladies if they wanted to go along, but they declined," General Hawkins said, and Fargo felt Alison's arm link into his. She led him away, and he found Brenda, Pearl, and Ida alongside him.

"It wouldn't have happened without you," Alison said. "We want to thank you, all of us. We thought we'd go back with you."

147

"A nice, slow trip." Brenda smiled.

"We all want a chance to thank you," Pearl said and Ida Bluebell smiled with quiet wisdom.

"We discussed it," Alison said. "We decided on it together. We'll make it a trip you'll remember." She pressed against him, and he felt Brenda at his other side, Pearl beside him, and Ida Bluebell's hand on the back of his neck.

"That damn Cheyenne was right. I'm either very brave and very wise or a fool on whom the gods have smiled," Fargo said. "I'll go with either."

LOOKING FORWARD!
The following is the opening
section from the next novel in the exciting
Trailsman series from Signet:

THE TRAILSMAN #180
THE GREENBACK TRAIL

Wyoming Territory, 1860,
where blue sky, purple peaks, and golden sun
were riches enough for most,
until the lure of green paper
turned one man's heart cold black . . .

He was almost asleep, stretched out on a sun-warmed rock and listening to the moan of the wind in the lodgepole pines and the gurgle of the stream down below, when he heard it. Or maybe it was too far away to hear, but that sixth sense he'd developed from years of living in the wilds had made him feel it. However it was, he somehow perceived the twang of a bow, the whistle of an arrow through the air, then the sharp sound of branches breaking. Not close, but close enough.

In one motion he rolled over onto his belly, the butt of his Colt suddenly in his hand, and peered over the edge

Excerpt from GREENBACK TRAIL

of the rock. Twenty feet down the tumbled rock slope, a brook glittered silver in the noonday sun, its occasional calm pools laden with the thick gold of spring pollen. His keen eyes shifted toward the crashing sound as a buck plunged out of the underbrush and staggered down the bank.

It was a superb creature with taut, muscular legs, a wide chest, a proud head, and many-pointed rack of antlers. The arrow in its ribs had sunk deep, almost to the feathers, and a trickle of blood darkened the tawny hide. The buck took a faltering step into the water and its knees gave way. It fell forward, then onto its side, nose barely above the rushing water. Fargo watched as the buck panted, then shuddered and the dark eyes went blank.

Skye Fargo tightened his finger on the trigger of his Colt and glanced behind him to where the black and white pinto stood tethered in the thicket of shadberry, almost invisible. His keen eyes swept the rocks, the pines, taking in the high blue Wyoming peaks sparkling with the last of the winter snow. No one. Nothing moving behind him. He shifted his gaze back to the scene below, wondering how many Shoshoni were in the hunting party. Shoshoni could be friendly to white men if they wanted. But sometimes they didn't want. Sometimes they got a bit testy when they caught white men passing through the little bit of territory they had left. It was just better to avoid the Shoshoni if you could. And here he was traveling alone through the Absaroka Range, many miles from any white settlement.

Fargo had just decided to slide down off the rock and retreat to the waiting Ovaro when a lone brave slipped out of the pines and ran toward the deer. Too late to move now. The Indian's sense of hearing was as acute as Fargo's. Any movement against the rock would be heard by the brave. There was nothing to do now but wait it out.

It was a Shoshoni—young, wiry, and muscular, and he moved as swiftly as the deer he had killed. With his fringed leather breeches he wore a white man's red plaid shirt. His braids were wound with several feathers. When he reached the dead buck, he stopped and then stood for a long moment, as if listening. His piercing black eyes swept the banks of the stream and then the edge of the woods. Fargo's finger was still tight on the trigger as he watched, wondering if the Shoshoni sensed he was being observed, felt his presence. How many more were with him?

After a long moment the brave shouldered his bow and drew a long knife from his belt. He glanced around one more time, uneasy, then fell to the task of butchering the buck. Fargo relaxed his trigger finger. The Shoshoni was alone. The best thing to do was to wait and watch, unmoving. The job would take a couple of hours, and then the Shoshoni would be on his way. From time to time Fargo kept an eye out behind him just in case. But there were no other Shoshoni to be seen.

The brave made short work of it with his knife and hatchet, expertly skinning the buck and rolling the beast out of its blood-wet hide, cutting the haunches and ribs into sections, and making packets of the various organ meats. Fargo admired the brave's butcher craft. It was not easy work to do fast, and even so it took a few hours. The buck's blood attracted a cloud of black flies that buzzed in the afternoon sun, and the spring wind carried the smell of blood to Fargo's nose. When the Shoshoni was nearly done, he laid his bow on the bank of the stream. He brought an appaloosa pony out of the woods and packed the meat onto a travois. He was kneeling next to the travois and tying the two hind haunches onto the pack when there came the sudden sound of movement from the bank of the stream just a few yards away.

The brave froze as a heavy, dark form rose out of the earth from the middle of a tangled copse. A terrifying roar split the silence as a gigantic grizzly bear shook its massive head and roared again.

In that instant Fargo realized the brave had been unlucky. He'd slain the buck just a few feet from the entrance to the bear's winter den. The smell of the fresh blood had awakened the grizzly, maddened with hunger after the long winter's sleep.

The Shoshoni took a step backward, fumbled for his bow, and then realized it was lying almost at the feet of the grizzly on the bank of the stream. Fargo could see the brave calculating his chances. His only chance was to run and abandon the horse and the butchered buck, hoping the bear would be distracted by the fresh meat. Suddenly the grizzly rushed, an enormous blur of brown and golden fur, of long black claws and teeth. The brave took off, but caught his foot in the stones of the bank, hitting the earth. The grizzly, attracted by the movement, lunged toward him.

Fargo's Colt spat fire. In rapid succession, one bullet through the side of the head, then another, then a third. There was no chance for the heart from this angle. The grizzly hurtled forward, throwing itself on top of the Shoshoni. Fargo aimed carefully, then plugged the massive skull again. The huge beast was sprawled half on the bank and half in the stream, the legs of the brave sticking out from one side. The Indian was struggling to get out from under the dying animal.

Fargo quickly reloaded his Colt, then donned his hat and went quickly down the side of the slope, fording the brook in long strides. By the time he reached the grizzly, it was in its final death throes, its sharp black claws scraping the earth, a deep shudder racking its huge body, and blood pouring from its eyes and mouth. The sound of its roar was indescribable. Fargo had seen many a man mauled badly by seemingly dying animals, and he wasn't about to be one of them. The bear, seeming to sense his presence, roused itself and took a swipe in his direction. Carefully aiming, so that the trajectory wouldn't kill the Shoshoni trapped underneath, Fargo put two more bullets through the bear's huge skull. The mountain of fur seemed to heave upward, as if the grizzly would rise to its feet, but it collapsed, lay still, and did not move again.

Fargo quickly wrenched one of the poles from the travois and jammed it under the grizzly, pushing upward. He threw his Colt onto the bank and knelt in the snowmelt of the brook to get a good angle. The icy water was up to his waist. The brave struggled and his bloody hands appeared, gripping the bear's fur as he tried to heave the huge corpse off. Fargo hefted again and the Shoshoni squirmed out from under the grizzly and scrambled instantly to his feet as he watched Fargo warily.

The brave had been hurt pretty badly, his right arm hanging loose and his shoulder bleeding where the bear had clawed and bit him. Two long claw marks scored one cheek—there'd be a helluva an impressive scar. But if Fargo hadn't been there, the brave would have been killed and they both knew it. He was a young man, compact and muscular, well suited for the hard life in the wilds. There was something generous and open in the brave's dark eyes. Fargo found himself liking the man immediately. He tried out a smile on the Indian. The Shoshoni regarded him silently, and his dark eyes shifted once as Fargo retrieved his Colt and holstered it.

"Friend," Fargo said, remembering the word in the Shoshoni tongue, which was a lot like what the Utes and the Hopis spoke. At the word the brave seemed very startled.

"Not many white men speak the tongue of the Snake People," the brave replied with a laugh of relief, referring to his tribe by the name the Plains Indians to the east used. "I am Istaga," he added. Fargo recognized the word for Coyote. This was Coyote-Man, and indeed, he had a wide grin like his canine namesake. "My people live to the north in the Land of Noise." Now Fargo grinned. Land of Noise? What the hell was that? He'd ask later.

"To my people, I am Skye Fargo, the Trailsman," he answered. "The Hopi call me Cloud-Man. The Navajo named me He-Who-Speaks-Fire. The Cheyenne call me Night-Walker."

"These are good names," Istaga said, obviously impressed. Fargo knew the importance of the ritual exchange of names to the various Indian people. "I have heard of you by many of these names. But I will call you Eagle-on-Wind."

To be named after the sacred eagle was a great honor. And Fargo was sure Istaga had come up with that name to commemorate the fact that Fargo had seemed to come out of nowhere, like an eagle from the sky.

"Let's get a fire going and your shoulder fixed up," Fargo said. He was suddenly aware he was chilled by the plunge into the icy water of the brook, and the late spring afternoon was turning brisk. Night would be coming in only a few hours. "Then we'll butcher this bear. I want you to show me how you got that deer cut up so quick."

"You were watching?" Istaga looked surprised. "You are quiet as . . . as . . ."

"An Eagle-on-Wind," Fargo cut in with a laugh.

Istaga laughed at that and they set to work. In a couple of hours, night was falling and they were sitting by a campfire, having feasted on fresh meat, wild onions and herbs, and a pot of coffee from Fargo's supplies. The rest of the buck and bear meat was packed and hanging a short distance away, suspended by ropes high above the ground so night-wandering animals couldn't get at it.

The Ovaro was tethered nearby, and Fargo had exchanged his damp clothes for some dry ones from his saddle bag and laid the wet contents of his pockets to dry out on a rock by the fire. Fargo had used mud from the brook and some torn fabric of an old shirt to bind up Istaga's wounds. The bites and claw marks were deep, and they must have hurt like hell, but through it all the Shoshoni hadn't winced. Fargo had admired the man's courage.

Now, with one arm bound in a sling and his shoulder bandaged, Istaga used his free hand to drink another cup of Fargo's coffee. He smacked his lips and wandered over to the rock to examine Fargo's belongings. Istaga picked up a double eagle and held it up glittering in the light.

"This is what the white man calls money," Istaga said thoughtfully. "Good to get a horse or tipi. But what good is this little sun except to trade?" He held the coin up again and looked at it curiously. "Maybe necklace? But bear claws better." He shrugged his one good shoulder and put the gold coin back on the rock again, then poked a pile of dollar bills, payment for the last job Fargo had done. Istaga looked up questioningly.

"That's money too," Fargo said. "Good for horses or a tipi." Istaga picked up one of the pieces of printed paper, waved it in the air, and laughed with delight.

"This good-for-nothing? I do not understand white men." Istaga picked up a dead leaf. "What if I decide to make this leaf good for a horse? Then I have money too. But this leaf is also good for nothing." He looked at the stack of dollar bills again, shaking his head in wonder.

Fargo grinned. The Indians were always amazed by the idea of money and, come to think of it, sometimes he found it pretty unbelievable too. Fargo took a swallow of hot coffee and watched as Istaga picked up another piece of paper that lay there. It was a letter. Even from across the campfire, Fargo could see the faint traces of ink that had been smeared and almost washed away by the water of the brook.

"This is money too?" Istaga asked.

"No," Fargo said. He stared into the fire for a long moment, watching the waves of darkness cross the bed of hot coals, thinking of the note he'd been carrying in his pocket. The ink might have been washed away in the brook, but he knew the words by heart. The message had reached him two months back. And ever since he'd been following a trail unlike any he'd ever tracked before. This time the trail wasn't marked by footprints in moist earth, broken branches, or crushed leaves. No, this time he'd been following rumors, half whispers, suspicion, and fear. The strange trail had taken him through the big spread of Nebraska and Utah territories, and into the land called Wyoming, from one two-bit town to the next, from the shabby office of a small-town banker to the glittering tawdriness of a high-class bordello. Two months on this curious trail, and all the time they'd been one step ahead of him. But now he felt like he was closing in on them. Yes, he'd have them cornered soon, the men he was chasing. Just a few more days, maybe tomorrow. And he'd find the man called Doug Simpkinson, the man who was waiting for him in Starkill. And together the two of them would do what had to be done. He felt Istaga's gaze on him, and he snapped out of his reverie. "No, that's not money," he said again.

"That's because the water took away the magic marks," Istaga said, muttering to himself. He carefully replaced the letter on the rock and looked down at the pile of dollar bills. "That is how white men know what is money."

Fargo smiled to himself at the Indian's logic. Istaga came closer to the fire and stirred it with a long stick. The sparks rose like tiny comets. A great horned owl gave five low hoots off in the distance. In the cool night the stars seemed close enough to touch.

"Where are the hunting lands for your tribe?" Fargo asked. "Where is this place you call the Land of Noise?"

In answer Istaga used a long stick to draw shapes in the earth by the campfire. Fargo recognized the shape of the Wind River, the Absaroka Range, and the Bighorn River. Istaga finally put the point of the stick on a place to the north.

"Home," the Shoshoni said.

Fargo knew the place. Most white men called it Colter's Hell after the tall Virginian, John Colter, who had trekked all alone through the area back in 1807 and reported back that the land there was filled with rivers that boiled and hillocks that spat great fountains of water and valleys that bubbled like caldrons. Most white men didn't believe Colter's stories, and few had had the courage to go and see for themselves. But Fargo had crossed through the area once, long years ago. He'd been in a hurry that time, riding for his life with a bunch of enraged Blackfoot on his tail, but he'd seen enough of Colter's Hell to know that John Colter had been telling the truth. The land there was as strange and mysterious as any he'd ever seen. And, remembering the hissing and gurgling, he understood why the Shoshoni called the place Land of Noise.

"No white men there," Istaga said. "Last place now with no white men."

Fargo heard the note of painful resignation in the brave's words. Yes, it was true. Every year prairie schooners came from the east, long lines of white-topped wagons bringing more settlers and homesteaders and ranchers who stopped somewhere and started cutting up the land, plowing and planting, building towns and roads and fences. The West was a helluva big place, but a man had to be blind not to see that one day the whole West was going to get filled up with white people. And Indians weren't blind. Every wagon brought them more trouble, another meaningless treaty, and less land. The territory called Colter's Hell, far from the mountain passes leading to Oregon and almost inaccessible among the formidable peaks, was one of the few places left that white men hadn't tried to lay claim to. Not yet, anyway.

Fargo rose and suggested they turn in. In a few minutes more, they were rolled up in their blankets. Fargo lay for a long time looking into the embers and thinking of the strange greenback trail he was following.

By dawn, they had struck camp and the horses were loaded, the travois packed with the bundled meat. Istaga tried to get Fargo to take some of the fresh meat for himself, but he refused all but a day's supply. Istaga was heading north, a half day's ride to the Land of Noise, and Fargo's trail led him due south to a little town called Starkill near the jagged Teton Peaks. As the sun tinged the tops of the snowy peaks pink, they led their horses along the bank of the brook until they intersected the north-south trail. There, Fargo raised his hand in a silent gesture, and Istaga did the same. Then the brave glanced up into the sky, grinned his Coyote grin, and pointed upward. Fargo saw a lone eagle flying high in the clear blue air. They nodded in farewell, and Fargo turned south with some regret. He'd met a lot of men while riding out in the West alone, Fargo thought, and Istaga the Coyote Man was one he'd have been happy to hunt with and ride with for a time.

It was a day's easy travel down to the town of Starkill. The big sky country of Wyoming Territory sped by beneath the pounding hooves of the powerful black and white pinto. The old trapper's trail arched up and down over the foothills of the Absaroka Range, through stands of lodgepole pines and stretches of dense scrub oak where green leaves were just unfolding in the warm spring air. Larks were reveling in the branches, and the land was full of big game—deer, elk, and moose. Far to the east, beyond his sight, across the high prairie ran the Bighorn River, swollen with fresh snowmelt. To the west, the range of snowy peaks pushed their heads against the blue sky. Hour after hour, the Trailsman rode, sometimes pausing to rest and water the Ovaro or stopping at a rise to survey the land ahead of him, to look for anything or anyone moving across the land.

Yeah, they were out there somewhere ahead of him. The men he'd been tracking for two long, wearying months. Dangerous men, armed to the teeth, a good two dozen as near as he could tell. And when he caught up to them, he wanted it to be a surprise. For them, not for him.

Fifteen miles north of Starkill, he stopped on a high ridge to scout out the pine forest in the valley below. The sun had slipped below a gray bank of clouds that hung low above the jagged fangs of the Teton Range. Then he saw it. His keen eyes were drawn to a movement. Something in a small yellow meadow that gleamed among the dark trees. Yes, there it was again. Riders crossing the open space, a good two miles away.

Fargo eased the Ovaro forward, guiding it off the trail to slip in among the dark trunks, moving forward at a quiet walk. The going was slow, but he knew right where they'd be. A few minutes later, he heard the shouts of men, a cackle of laughter, and a sharp cry. They were just ahead. Fargo halted the pinto and slid down, gliding forward on foot, silent as a snake over the thick carpet of pine needles, eyes and ears alert.

The shouting and laughter grew louder, along with the whinny of a horse echoing through the forest. Movement ahead. Horses and three men standing guard, wary, looking out into the trees, their rifles at the ready. They were being damn careful, he could see that. He shrank back and made a wide circle through the trees, approaching from the other side. He wished he had hooked up with Doug Simpkinson already—hell, there wasn't much he could do alone. He slowly circled in again, and he saw more guards, a line of watchful men. But beyond them, through the trees, he could spot a crowd of other men. With all those men on guard, it was impossible to get closer or to see what they were up to. There was shouting, but he was too far away to make out the words. Then came the sound of another man's shout of anger, defiance, and—yes—fear. A roar of raucous laughter, the pop of three gunshots in quick succession. Fargo swore softly to himself, fury rising in him. There wasn't a damn thing he could do against two dozen men. And whoever had just been murdered—and he had no doubt that's what had happened there among the dense tree trunks—it was too late now to save him. He waited for another twenty minutes, hoping the men would move out so he could slip in and see what had happened. But then he saw the rising smoke of a campfire, and he realized the men were going to stay there the night.

Fargo backed away, melted into the shadows of the forest, and returned to where the Ovaro waited. He mounted, sat for a moment listening to the distant sounds of the men, uttered a silent curse, and rode back to the trail. Yeah, it was them, all right. The men he'd been seeking. His fists tightened on the reins until his knuckles grew white and his fingers hurt. He noticed and loosened them, pushing his fury deep within, storing it up for the time when he'd get his revenge. It would be soon. And it would be sweet.

On the final stretch on the trail into Starkill, the sun slipped out from beneath the thick clouds and hung over the peaks in a blaze of golden glory. Fargo stopped to admire the spectacular sunset, splashed with scarlet, fiery apricot, and burnished bronze. He was looking westward across a grassy meadow pocked with wild-flowers when a puff of white smoke rose from just over the lip of a hill, as if somebody—somebody not very good at it—had just started a campfire. Fargo started to move on, but then thought of the desperate men he'd left a few miles behind him in the forest and what they might do to anybody they caught out in the open. The town of Starkill was just two miles down the road. Why the hell was somebody camping out here when they could get into town?

Fargo cantered across the meadow as the colors in the sky above deepened and grew richer by the minute—one of the most beautiful sunsets he'd ever seen, and he'd seen some beauts.

As Fargo came up over the top of the hill, he laughed out loud at what he saw. An old man with a long white beard and wearing a black beret stood in front of an easel that held a square of canvas on which was a half-finished picture of the sunset. With one hand the old man held a round wooden palette on which were daubs of bright colors, and with the other he brandished a long brush.

Nearby was a badly staked canvas tent that he was sure would collapse at a mere gust of night breeze. Two broken-down nags were tied to a bush so loosely they could pull away at the slightest scare. A lithe figure in a cherry red dress knelt over the smoking campfire, her face hidden from his gaze by a wide straw hat with a bunch of just picked wildflowers on top. She was laying green branches over the fire, and white smoke was rising in billows.

At the sound of Fargo's laugh and the creak of the saddle, the woman looked up. In an instant he took in a host of impressions. She was beautiful, her thick auburn hair falling in soft waves over her shoulders to her waist, her lips rosy against her pale skin, eyes blue as clear sky. The high collar and long sleeves of her dress couldn't disguise her slender figure with her high, full breasts and narrow waist. But she was no mere girl, and in her expression was a mixture of innocence and also a long-carried burden, something that weighed her down. He guessed her age at about thirty and noticed she wasn't wearing a wedding ring. A nice-looking woman like her should have settled down long ago. He wondered what her story was.

Fargo dismounted and walked toward her. She stood up, pine branches in hand. The old man didn't seem to take any notice of his arrival, but continued to daub paint hurriedly onto the canvas, as if to capture the sunset before it faded away.

"You trying to make a smoke signal?" Fargo asked her, nodding toward the smoking fire.

"Just a campfire," she said, blushing. Fargo bent down and removed the green boughs from the tiny fire, replacing them with some dry grass and branches. In a moment it blazed up, almost smokeless.

"Oh, that's better," she said, flashing him a smile. "Thank you. My name's Bethany. That's my pa, Asa. Asa—Dalrimple." She gestured to the old man, who was engrossed in his painting. Asa waved his brush over his shoulder, indicating he was aware of the new arrival but couldn't stop painting or take his eyes off the sunset. Bethany shifted from foot to foot nervously. Yeah, she should be nervous, he thought. He could be anybody coming upon them in the middle of the meadow. The two of them were the greenest tenderhorns he'd ever seen camping out in the West. Sitting ducks for whatever kind of trouble might come along, whether from nature or from other men.

"My name's Skye Fargo," he said as he extended his hand. She shyly took it, her delicate hand warm in his for just a moment.

"Skye Fargo," she said. "What a nice name." Unlike most people in the West, she didn't recognize his name, hadn't heard the stories that were told throughout the territories. From the paleness of her skin and her clothing, Fargo figured she'd spent her life back East.

"I don't mean to pry, but are you planning on spending the night here?"

"We're heading toward a town called Starkill," Bethany answered. "I guess we'll get there tomorrow."

"Just some advice from a stranger," Fargo said. "I'd get into town tonight, find a good hotel room. Camping in the wilds is fine when you know what you're doing." He lightly toed the wobbly stake that was holding one corner of the tent, and at the slight pressure it pulled loose and the tent collapsed.

Bethany's mouth formed a silent "Oh." Her blue eyes followed him as he approached the two old nags and retied them more securely to a chokecherry bush.

"*Voilà!*" Asa Dalrimple's voice rang out as he stepped

back from the canvas and twirled his brush in the air. Fargo walked over to take a look. It was a helluva nice picture. The sunset had faded to red and gray above the Tetons, but on the rectangle of canvas Asa had managed to capture it in all its glory. The old man had got the colors just right and the tall snowy peaks that seemed to gnaw at the clouds.

"You interested in buying a painting?" Dalrimple asked as he started cleaning his brush with a rag full of pungent turpentine.

"If I was, I'd buy this one," Fargo answered truthfully. It was damn good. "But I've got no place to hang it. And besides, I get a free sunset every evening. Every night a different picture."

"Talk like that would put us artists out of business," Dalrimple said with a laugh, wiping his palette clean and packing his tools away in a wooden case. He carefully removed the wet oil painting and handed it to Bethany, who propped it up on a rock. Then he folded up the easel and, wiping his hands on his rag, he turned to Fargo.

Asa Dalrimple's blue eyes were sharp over his thick white beard. They shone with humor and intelligence. But there was also suffering there, Fargo saw. Beneath his beret the old man wore his white hair long too, like those European artist types. His battered black frock coat was cut in a loose flowing style, and he'd knotted a wild purple scarf around the neck of his shirt.

"Now, who might you be?" Dalrimple asked.

"The name's Skye Fargo." There was a flicker of recognition in the old man's eyes, interest and . . . wariness. But his face betrayed nothing. Neither did his words.

"Nice to meet you, sir."

"I was just suggesting to your daughter that you get into town for the night," Fargo said. He hesitated a moment before deciding what to say next. On one hand, he wanted to impress on these two incompetents that there were dangers out here—like two dozen armed and desperate men. On the other hand, his instinct told him not to tip his hand about what he knew and his reason for being there. Chances were, the men he'd left behind in the forest would stay put for the night, but why take the chance? "You'd be more comfortable in a good hotel," he said at last.

"But Starkill's the next town, and it's thirty miles up the road," Bethany said, coming up to them. "Why, we wouldn't get there till tomorrow morning."

"You're practically on top of it. Starkill's two miles over that next hill," Fargo said, trying to keep from rolling his eyes. Asa and Bethany looked at each other in surprise and delight. The two tenderhorns didn't even know where the hell they were. "Come on, I'll help you get packed and take you there."

A half hour later, just as the last of the light was leaving the western sky, they rode into Starkill. It wasn't much of a town. Here and there oil lamps hanging from the eaves of the stores lit the scene dimly. The false-fronted stores lined the dusty main street, and beyond them were some sod houses and a couple of tents pitched on the back streets. There wasn't even much of a saloon, just a small open-fronted store with a sign that read DRINKING. Another joint was called THE EATERY, and inside the window he could see people gathered around rude tables inside. Starkill was a hardscrabble community on the edge of wilderness, and there weren't many folks out on the streets.

The few folks he saw in passing wagons and on the boardwalks wore simple clothes of homespun and sheepskin. From what he observed, he knew immediately that most of the locals were ranchers. He'd seen scores of towns like this one, and he knew the kind of life ranchers led. To carve out your own ranch meant battling the blasting heat of summer when your cattle went thirsty and their black tongues hung out of their mouths, and fighting the winter ice storms when your herd froze like statues. It was a damn hard life. Only the toughest survived. It was clear that nobody around Starkill was making much of a living, if you counted it in money. But they were making a good life. Over and over again he saw the few men and women greeting one another and stopping to talk and pass on gossip. It seemed like a friendly and close-knit community.

As they rode through, nearly everybody they passed stopped to stare openly at the three of them, less at Fargo's tall frame atop his black and white pinto than at Asa Dalrimple in his beret and purple scarf, his easel strapped to the side of his horse. And especially, the men in particular, stared at Bethany and her extravagant red hair and cherry-colored frock.

At the end of the street, he spotted a sign that read ROOMS. They dismounted and tethered the horses. Inside, an ample, grandmotherly-looking woman with a knot of gray hair signed them into the guest register and then prepared to lead them up the narrow stairs to show them their rooms.

"I'm going to stable the horses first," Fargo said, pocketing his room key. He was eager to get on with business. There was no time to lose.

"Oh," Bethany said, turning about on the stairway. Her father and the landlady continued up the stairs. Bethany wasn't trying to hide the disappointment in her blue eyes. "But I thought . . . maybe you'd join us for dinner, Mr. Fargo." Her fingers played with the top button of her high-necked dress. "After all, I—my Pa and I—owe you thanks for getting us into town."

Fargo smiled, wondering just how grateful she'd be. She was hard to read, seeming so innocent yet with that mysterious something that he couldn't quite put his finger on.

"Well, if you're over at the Eatery later, I'll look in on you," he said. "Or I'll see you around tomorrow."

"Are you going to be in town long?" Bethany asked. She stepped down one step and came up close to him.

Fargo reached out one arm and wrapped it around her waist, drawing her close. She came willingly, pliant as a green willow, as he bent to kiss her lightly, just brushing his lips against hers, inhaling the warm perfume of her that rose from her neck, her thick hair. Then he let her go. She blushed uncertainly and held onto the railing.

"Yeah, I'll be around a few days at least," he said lightly. He touched the brim of his hat and stepped out into the night. Horses first. He led their three mounts to a stable he'd spotted just off the main street. After inspecting the stalls and the oat bins, he was satisfied the Ovaro would be well taken care of. Then he walked to the main street and retraced his steps to a storefront he'd passed on the way in. The sign read STARKILL SHERIFF. The windows were dark. Fargo knocked anyway. No sound inside. He looked around. A group of passing ranchmen paused when they spotted him, and Fargo nodded a greeting.

"I'm looking for the sheriff," he said. "Anybody know where he's at?"

"Sure, stranger," one of the men said. "At this hour you can always find him having dinner over there." He jerked his thumb toward the Eatery.

Fargo crossed the street and walked into the crowded room. Rustic wooden tables and chairs took up most of the space. At one end of the room was a giant stone fireplace where gobbets of meat were sizzling on spits and a row of pots steamed the spicy odor of bean chili. A rotund bald man with a big smile and half his teeth missing hurried by with a tray of grilled steaks. Fargo figured he was the proprietor and signaled to him on his way back to the kitchen.

"I'm Eddie Bly, proprietor of this here establishment," the bald man said in a booming voice as he paused to wipe his hands on his white apron. "Can I get you some grub, stranger?"

"I'm looking for the sheriff," Fargo shouted over the hubbub.

"Sheriff? He's here every night," the rotund man shouted back with his gap-toothed smile, "sits right over . . ." He started to point at a small table in the corner, but it was empty. The man scanned the room once, then twice, a puzzled look on his face. He glanced at the large clock on the wall, then scratched his head. "That's strange," he said in a low voice that Fargo almost didn't catch above the noise. "That's strange—" he said again, louder for Fargo's benefit. "Sheriff Doug Simpkinson ain't never missed dinner here in four years." The proprietor was called by one of his customers, and as he moved away, he glanced back over his shoulder once again to the empty spot where the sheriff usually sat.

Fargo walked out of the Eatery into the cool night air. For the next half hour he checked the drinking establishment and every store, careful to give some innocuous excuse for wanting to find the sheriff so as not to cause alarm or get tongues wagging. But Sheriff Doug Simpkinson was nowhere to be found. At least nowhere in Starkill.

As Fargo stood on the boardwalk in front of the sheriff's office, he gazed down the quiet streets of the town of Starkill. He thought of the men in the forest. There was big trouble coming to this little town. Like an echo, he heard the men's raucous laughter and the one man's voice that had cried out in defiance, in anger, in fear. Then the three gunshots. Yeah. Could be. It could be that it had been Sheriff Doug Simpkinson in the forest that afternoon, murdered by those men. Fargo swore silently. And if Simpkinson had been killed, then he was now in this all alone. He felt the weight of the secret he'd sworn not to tell. And now he was one man against a couple dozen. Yeah, big trouble was heading to the town of Starkill.

WHISPERS OF THE MOUNTAIN
BY TOM HRON

The Indians of Alaska gave the name Denali to the great sacred
mountain they said would protect them from anyone who tried to
take the vast wilderness from them. But now white men had come
to Denali, looking for the vast lode of gold that legend said was
hidden on its heights. A shaman lay dead at the hands of a greed-
mad murderer, his wife was captive to this human monster, and his
little daughter braved the frozen wasteland to seek help. What she
found was lawman Eli Bonnet, who dealt out justice with his gun,
and Hannah, a woman as savvy a survivor as any man. Now in the
deadly depth of winter, a new hunt began on the treacherous slopes
of Denali—not for gold but for the most dangerous game of all....

from **SIGNET**

Prices slightly higher in Canada.   (0-451-187946—$5.99)

WAR EAGLES
BY FRANK BURLESON

In the North, a lanky lawyer named Abraham Lincoln was recovering from a brutal political setback. In the South, eloquent U.S. Senator Jefferson Davis was risking all in a race for governor of his native Mississippi. And far to the Southwest, the future of the frontier was being decided as the U.S. Army, under Colonel Bull Moose Sumner, faced the growing alliance of Native Americans led by the great Mangus Colorados and determined to defend their ancestral lands. For First Lieutenant Nathanial Barrington it was his first test as a professional soldier following orders he distrusted in an undeclared war without conscience or quarter—and his test as a man when he met the Apache woman warrior Jocita in a night lit by passion that would yield to a day of dark decision . . .

from **SIGNET**

Prices slightly higher in Canada.   (0-451-18090-9—$4.50)
